William Faulkner

Annotations to the Novels

Edited by
James B. Meriwether
University of South Carolina

Advisory Editor
Dianne Luce

A GARLAND SERIES

The Garland Faulkner Annotation Series

Series Editor: James B. Meriwether
Advisory Editor: Dianne Luce

PYLON

Annotated by
Susie Paul Johnson

Garland Publishing, Inc.
New York & London
1989

Copyright © 1989 by Susie Paul Johnson
All Rights Reserved

Library of Congress Cataloging-in-Publication Data

Johnson, Susie Paul.
Pylon/ annotated by Susie Paul Johnson.
p. cm.—(William Faulkner: annotations to the novels)
ISBN 0-8240-4231-X (alk. paper)
1. Faulkner, William, 1897–1962. Pylon. I. Faulkner,
William, 1897–1962. Pylon. II. Title. III. Series.
PS3511.A86P9535 1989   89-33876
813'.52—dc20

The volumes in this series have been printed on
acid-free, 250-year-life paper.

Manufactured in the United States of America

For my mother and father

Preface by Series Editor

The annotations in the volumes of this series are intended to assist the reader of Faulkner's novels to understand obscure or difficult words and passages, including literary allusions, dialect, and historical events that Faulkner uses or alludes to in the twenty works included. The scope of these annotations varies, necessarily, from volume to volume. But throughout the series the goal has been to provide useful, brief explanations or definitions for what may be puzzling in Faulkner's text.

Obviously what is puzzling to one reader may be clear to another, and these annotations are provided for a varied and changing audience. For many readers today, especially those from the American South, explanations of dialect words and spellings may be unnecessary. The same may be true of many of the historical and geographical annotations. But with the passage of time, a steadily increasing percentage of Faulkner's readers will need help with such points, and what may be foreign today only to Faulkner's readers from other countries, will be increasingly foreign to American readers in the years to come.

Though the annotations have usually been kept brief, each volume is intended to be inclusive, and useful independently of the others. As a rule words that can be found in standard unabridged dictionaries are not annotated, but this rule has not been followed consistently. Usefulness and clarity rather than consistency have been the criteria for this series.

The pioneering work in this field was Calvin Brown's *A Glossary of Faulkner's South* (Yale University Press, 1976). Though our volumes obviously can go into very much greater detail than could Professor Brown's book, almost every volume in this series is indebted to his more substantially than the acknowledgments for individual annotations can show. Even when we have expanded, corrected, or disagreed with him, we have always been conscious of how much this series owes to his knowledge and his labors.

All those involved in this project are fully aware that no such endeavor can ever be complete or difinitive. Further close reading of Faulkner's texts and further study of his sources and influences will reveal new allusions. Further linguistic research will provide additional information about his use of dialect. Such progress in the study of Faulkner will be never-ending, with obvious consequences for such reference works as these. Accordingly, in order to correct and update the information provided in these volumes, there will be a regular department in the *Mississippi Quarterly* devoted to notes and queries, addenda and corrigenda, concerning these annotations.

J.B.M.

Introduction

These annotations are intended to serve as a companion to *Pylon*, Faulkner's 1935 story of barnstorming flyers and the reporter who becomes obsessed with them, a novel that rewards such close reading. This volume documents the details of real places, characters, and events Faulkner includes; explains and offers historical and technical background for references to aircraft and aviation; defines slang and explains topical references from the 1930s; notes echoes of other works by Faulkner or of works by authors he read or might have read; and restores the profanity excised from the novel by an editor.

Pylon takes place at an airshow very much like the one Faulkner attended in February of 1934, during Carnival in New Orleans, a city where he had lived from January to June of 1925 (Blotner 385–431). As Michael Millgate, Cleanth Brooks, and Joseph Blotner have already demonstrated, and as these annotations further show, the novel draws heavily on the airshow, the city, and its celebration of Mardi Gras for its setting, and, to a lesser extent, for its characters and action. The year before, on February 2, 1933, Faulkner had begun taking formal instruction in flying from Vernon Omlie, a flight instructor during the War and one-time barnstormer who had started Mid-South Airways in Memphis in 1922 (Blotner 796). Faulkner had not only earned his pilot's license, but bought his own plane, a Waco C cabin cruiser, and, in April of 1934, sponsored an airshow in Ripley, Mississippi—"William Faulkner's Air Circus" (Blotner 831, 842). His involvement with flying and his knowledge of aircraft are evident in *Pylon*'s subject matter, of course, but also in the abundance of references, some of which are archaic now, to airplanes and flying, including barnstorming, air racing, and stunt flying. This volume defends these terms, and through cross-referencing and commentary within each note, attempts to offer a coherent picture of aviation in the thirties—background that can enrich a reader's pleasure in an understanding of the novel. The research for this group of annotations—which involved interviewing experts as well as consulting aviation dictionaries and histories, many contemporary with the novel—was completed in 1983, before Robert Harrison published *Aviation Lore in Faulkner* (1985). Their accuracy has since been confirmed by his work.

Pylon is rich in the variety of its language; thus many other works and specialized terms are here explained to aid readers as they make their way through the argot of aviation, as well as southern colloquialisms, various dialects, newspaper jargon, the invented compound words of the narrator, and the hard-edged slang and occasional reference to the bureaucracy and government programs of the the Depression.

Especially because of its subject and its urban setting, this novel seems, at least initially, an anomaly among Faulkner's works; yet it is connected to them in many ways and reflects the same basic concerns as the Yoknapatawpha novels and stories. Noted here are echoes in *Pylon* of other works by Faulkner from very early in his career through *The Hamlet* (1940). Predictably the novel echoes others concerned with flyers, like *Soldiers' Pay* and *Flags in the Dust*, and those works set in New Orleans, like *Elmer, Mosquitoes*, or *The Wild Palms*. Included here too are allusions to those works that Faulkner wrote or revised within three or four years of *Pylon*—like *Sanctuary, Light in August*, one poem in *A Green Bough*, and the stories that first appeared in periodicals before Faulkner revised them, added a concluding chapter, and published them as *The Unvanquished*. Though there are references to Quentin and *The Sound and the Fury*, overt references to *Absalom, Absalom!*, which Faulkner put down to work on *Pylon*, are absent (Gwyn and Blotner 36). Apparently *Pylon* did offer him the reprieve he needed from the other novel.

Also identified in these annotations are Faulkner's references to other authors' works, including direct allusions to T. S. Eliot's poetry—in particular, to "Preludes," "The Love Song of J. Alfred Prufrock," "The Waste Land," and "The Hollow Men"; scattered references to other modernist poets like Conrad Aiken, Ezra Pound, and e. e. cummings; to novelists James Joyce, John Dos Passos, and Sherwood Anderson; to two war novels Faulkner knew, Elliot White Springs' *War Birds* and *Under Fire* by Henri Barbusse; to Shakespeare, the Bible, and to one of Faulkner's admitted favorites, *Don Quixote* (Gwyn and Blotner 50); to Freud, whom Faulkner claimed not to have read, and to another kind of determinist he is known to have read, Louis Berman.

Full bibliographical citations to literary, critical, historical, and reference works are given within the note at the first appearence of each; subsequent references are cited in shortened form. Dates of publication for those works discussed but not quoted are provided at the first mention of the work only, though full citations appear in the bibliography. As this is a reference rather than a critical work, most of the annotations are factual rather than interpretive, except where criticism and interpretation are necessary to justify the note.

Relative to the attention given much of Faulkner's work, *Pylon* has been largely neglected. Yet these annotations not only document this novel's richness, they also suggest fresh critical directions. Perhaps *Pylon* will soon receive the re-evaluation of which it is so worthy.

Susie Paul Johnson

Pylon (title): Pylons are the towers which mark the turning points in air races, usually "slender structures of wood or steel covered with brightly-colored cloth panels and surmounted by flags" (Robert Harrison, Aviation Lore in Faulkner [Amsterdam: Benjamins, 1985] 154). In ancient Egyptian architecture, they are the "rectangular, truncated, pyramidal towers flanking the gateway of a temple" (Nikolaus Pevsner, et. al., A Dictionary of American Architecture [Woodstock, NY: Overlook, 1976] 405). Thus, André Bleikasten, who sees the title as one of a series of references to Egypt, defines pylon at the beginning of his article on the novel: "Pylône: Portail monumental placé à l'entrée des temples egyptiens encadré de deux massifs de maconnerie en forme de pyramide tronquee dont les faces entaient couvertes de peintures et d'inscriptions. Le Petit Robert" ("Pylon, Ou L'enfer des Signes," Études Anglaises 29[1976]: 437). Michel Gresset describes the pylon as "l'objet phallique, le point de mire" ("Théorème," Recherches Anglaises et Americaines 9[1976]: 78). Joseph McElrath argues that Faulkner chose "a pylon, not pylons, as the initial image for his novel" because "there is a singular focal object, Laverne Shumann" ("Pylon: The Portrait of a Lady," Mississippi Quarterly 27[1974]: 276).

7.1 Jiggs: Blotner points out that Jiggs resembles the airplane mechanic in "Mythical Latin-American Kingdom Story" (Faulkner: A Biography [New York: Random House, 1974] 866), a story which Faulkner suggested to Sam Marx at MGM in 1933 (800). The more famous Jiggs is, of course, Father in George McManus' comic strip, Bringing Up Father, which originated around 1915. He is an Irish immigrant who has become wealthy, but still yearns "only for a night out with his old cronies at Dinty Moore's" (Jerry Robinson, The Comics: An Illustrated History of Comic Strip Art [New York: Putnam's, 1974] 57). What the two Jiggs share are wives they wish to escape. McManus' Jiggs flees his money- and status-hungry wife at the local pub; Faulkner's Jiggs has fled to New Orleans and elsewhere. He explains, "Everytime I did a job her or the sheriff would catch the guy and get the money before I could tell him I was through" (Pylon [New York: Harrison Smith and Robert Haas, 1935] 16; P hereafter).

7.2 light spatter of last night's confetti: The first reference to the Carnival celebration in progress. Actually, it is unlikely that confetti would have been part of the debris littering the streets after a parade. Confetti has never become a part of New Orleans' Mardi Gras (Robert Tallant, Mardi Gras [Garden City, NY: Doubleday, 1948] 116), yet the spatter of confetti allows Faulkner the comparison to "spent dirty foam" in the next line and to "rain" (e.g. 57). The drifting confetti and serpentine are a repeated image in Pylon (see also note 77.13-16), akin perhaps to the debris in Conrad Aiken's "Episode in Grey," in Nocturne of Remembered Spring, first published in Boston by Four Seas, 1917: "So, to begin with, dust blows down the street,/ In lazy clouds and swirls, and after that/ Tatters of paper and straws, and waves of heat,/ And leaves plague-bitten" (Collected Poems [New York: Oxford UP, 1970] 21). Debris blown about by the wind is a repeated image in Sherwood Anderson's Marching Men (1917): "In the little court under the window lay heaps of discarded newspaper tossed about by the wind . . . . On hot evenings he laid down his book and, leaning for out of the window, rubbed his eyes and watched the discarded newspapers, sorried by the whirlpools of wind in the court, run here and there, dashing against the warehouse walls and vainly trying to escape over the roof . . . . He began to think that the lives of most of the people about him were much like the dirty newspaper" ([Cleveland: Case Western Reserve UP, 1972] 56).

7.3 windowbase: The first of many compound words of Faulkner's invention. Many critics--like Edmond Volpe, who calls these words "Joycean wordmergers" (A Reader's Guide to William Faulkner [New York: Farrar, Straus and Giroux, 1964] 175)--suggest that Faulkner learned this technique from Joyce. James Meriwether suggests that Dos Passos--whom Faulkner frequently named as an "important contemporary" (Lion in the Garden: Interviews with William Faulkner, 1926-1962, eds. James B. Meriwether and Michael Millgate [New York: Random House, 1968] 58)--is a more likely source. Though not as often as Faulkner does in Pylon, Dos Passos creates compound words in <u>Manhattan Transfer</u> (1925) and in the "Camera Eye" sections of <u>The 42nd Parallel</u> (1930) and <u>1919</u> (1932). Another word in the same line--"lightpoised"-- is closer to what Hugh Ruppersburg describes as an "elliptical" image which fuses "at least two, frequently contradictory, words into a single expression," evoking "vivid visual impressions by implying much more than they say outright" (<u>Voice and Eye in Faulkner's Fiction</u> [Athens: U of Georgia P, 1983] 59). These compound words not only "express the individual observer's unique perceptions" and "connote the oxymoronic character of New Valois," but "intensify mood," the intensity of a scene's tone and impact varying "directly in proportion to elliptical imagery's frequency of occurrence" (59).

7.3 spent dirty foam: The first of many references to the sea or water: for example, confetti and serpentine are rain (53, 57, 77, 201); crowds are streams and tides (37, 140, 147); a building "floats," a car "drifts," a train station "flows up," the city "dissolves," (16, 88, 213, 267); New Valois (see note 14.18) is surrounded by swamp and "outraged" lake (11, 30); the air is humid (15 and note 15.24-26); finally, Roger drowns in Lake Rambaud (see note 14.25-26; <u>P</u> 234), and the reporter lives on Noyades (184 and note 184.25), the street of the drowned. Michael Millgate suggests that for the poetic technique of the novel, the "aiming at the establishment of a total pattern of imagery through an almost obssessive recurrence of significant phrases, symbols, places, objects," Faulkner is indebted to Eliot's "The Waste Land" (The Achievement of William Faulkner [Lincoln: U of Nebraska P, 1978] 144). Specifically, the water and Shumann's "death by water" suggest Eliot (Millgate 144 and Richard P. Adams, Faulkner: Myth and Motion [Princeton: Princeton UP, 1968] 101). Without reference to Eliot, Ruppersburg describes this repetition of images as "as important a structural element as point of view and . . . a more powerful force in the narrative . . . a form of symbolism reinforcing Faulkner's portrayal of a modern world mired in decay and atrophy" (59).

7.5-7 boots . . . inviolate implication of horse and spur: "The mystique linking the worlds of aeroplanes and horses, born in the earliest days of military aviation, did not die easily," according to Robert Harrison. In the 1930s, Roscoe Turner was the living embodiment of the air ace, "large, moustachioed . . . clad in flared calvary breeches and Savile Row riding boots (154). Perhaps also an allusion to Pegasus, the winged horse Bellerophon rode when he destroyed Chimaera.

7.5 slantshimmered: References to light are even more frequent than references to water (see note 7.3, "spent dirty foam"). The novel describes unnatural light--"unearthly" "sourceless," "gray palpable . . . without weight or light" (7, 37, 110); the shapes light cuts--"downfunnelled,"

"outfalling," "round target," "lightpoint," "savage bars,"
"fingers" (41, 58, 75, 261, 262, 283); light as it effects or
catches an image--"earth dragged . . . into air and
alternations of light," "that crosssection out of timespace
as though of a lightray caught by a speed lens," "caught for
a second in a lightbeam," "light carrying the image" (30, 75,
77, 193); light and mechanism--"ordered and marked by light
and bell," "waiting for the same clock," "the long sicklebar
of the beacon" sweeping "with clocklike and deliberate
precision," "green and red and white electrics waned and
pulsed and flicked" (77, 176, 252, 283). Ruppersburg
describes the airport beacon light as a static image
"signifying the deadening inertia and artificiality of New
Valois" (60).

7.10-11 purple-and-gold tissue bunting: First indication that
a Carnival (see note 7.2) celebration, specifically, is in
progress, as purple and gold, along with green, are the
official Carnival colors--"green for faith, gold for power
and purple for justice" (Laurraine Goreau, "Mardi Gras," The
Past as Prelude: New Orleans 1718-1968, ed. Hodding Carter,
Jr. [New Orleans: Tulane UP, 1968] 355). However, the color
green for faith and for the spring, which the Carnival ushers
in and which Laverne's name suggests, is notably absent
throughout Pylon. Cf. "Wealthy Jew, " New Orleans Sketches:
"I love three things: gold; marble and purple" (Ed. Purnel
Collins [New York: Random House, 1958] 3).

7.13 aeroplanes: Faulkner is using the British spelling, a vestige of his time as a Royal Air Force recruit in Canada, perhaps. In the galley proofs, now held by the Harry Ransom Humanities Research Center, University of Texas at Austin, a proofreader has Americanized the spelling. The correction has been crossed through probably by Faulkner's editor Hal Smith, who brought the Pylon galleys to Oxford and may have worked through them with Faulkner (Selected Letters of William Faulkner, ed. Joseph Blotner [New York: Vintage, 1978] 88). Two pages over, however, Jiggs uses the word "airplane," as does the reporter (48). A proofreader has noted this second spelling. Again, the query is marked through, so the American spelling remains in these instances. The British spelling (and pronunciation) is the narrator's; the American spelling, the characters'. It is interesting that Faulkner has approved the proofreader's Americanization of his spelling of "amplifyer," perhaps because this is not an audible difference (see note 23.21).

7.15-16 aeroplanes . . . a species of . . . animals: Throughout Pylon mechanical objects are characterized as animal, people as animal and mechanical. The reporter describes the flyers as not human, the child "dropped already running like a colt or a calf from the fuselage of an airplane (48), all of them with "cylinder oil" instead of blood (45). Jiggs has legs like a "polo pony's" (8), but is also compared to "tautly sprung steel" (146); the airplane's "spare entrails revealed" suggest "the halfeaten carcass of a deer" (19), "lying on its back, the undercarriage projecting into the air," the plane is later compared to "a dead bird" (164); small boats are "butterflies," the dredgeboat is "something antediluvian" which crawls, the police launch a "vegetarian whale" (237, 252).

8.8 Yair: Roger's, Jack's, and especially Jiggs' version of yes, which the reporter picks up and begins to use constantly. It punctuates his breathless conversation with his editor (42-51) or, along with "yah," his private thoughts (61-63). One slang dictionary lists yair, describing it as 20th-century Australian illiterate (Eric Partridge, comp., A Dictionary of Slang and Unconventional English, 7th ed. [New York: MacMillan, 1970] 1521), but whatever its origin, Faulkner makes it unique in this novel to this small group of flyers.

10.6-7 like watching the ostrich in the movie cartoon swallow the alarm clock: The first of several references to stage and film, comedy especially: "the scene began to resemble that comic stage one where the entire army enters one taxicab and drives away" (15); "like the comedy young bachelor caught by his girl while holding a strange infant on a street corner" (36); "they resembled the tall and the short man of the orthodox and unfailing comic team" (56); "like burlesqued internes in comedies" (88): "that atmosphere of a fifteenth century Florentine stage scene" (167-168); "the cartoon comedy centaur" (270); "that burlesque outrage and despair of the spontaneous amateur buffoon" (288); "Where do mules and vaudeville acts go?" (291); "a bungalow . . . which California moving picture films have scattered across North America as if the celluloid carried germs" (304).

11.19 Grandlieu Street: Cleanth Brooks identifies this as Canal Street ("Notes: Place Names in Pylon," William Faulkner: Toward Yoknapatawpha and Beyond [New Haven: Yale UP, 1978] 408), New Orleans' main street. Jiggs is directed to Grandlieu by a clerk in the store where he eventually buys his hew boots when he asks where to catch a bus. Most street cars and many bus lines begin and end at Canal, a street that became the town commons, dividing the old city on the downtown side from the newer uptown section, when the shallow canal for which it was named was filled in (Federal Writers' Project, Lyle Saxon, dir., New Orleans City Guide [Boston: Houghton Mifflin, 1938] 286).

11.25-26 bayou and swampsuspired air: Surrounded by swamps and low-lying delta lands, New Orleans is a humid place. The New Orleans City Guide describes it as an urban oasis lying in a dike-enclosed area between the Mississippi River and Lake Pontchartrain. . . . The average elevation of the city, in fact, which is below the high-water levels of both the

Mississippi River and Lake Pontchartrain, is but one foot above mean Gulf level" (3). Bayous--which are natural canals, "flood distributaries and drainage streams for swamps--make up a drainage network for the state" (Federal Writers' Program, Lyle Saxon, state sup., Louisiana: A Guide to the State [New York: Hastings, 1941] 9).

11.27 windrows against wallangles: The first of many references to lines, angles, tunnels--as if the city were a labyrinth or maze: "aerial and bottomless regalcolored cattlechute suspended," "grass labyrinthed by concrete driveways," "a narrow alley like a gutter," "into the dark mouth of the street now so narrow of curb that they followed in single file," "two narrow roofless tunnels like exposed minegalleries," "that quarter of narrow canyons, the exposed minegalleries hung with iron lace," "through a dark canyon of mosshung liveoaks," "one of ten thousand narrow tunnels furnished with a counter," "the reporter thought of a man trying to herd a half dozen blind sheep through a passage a little wider than he could span with his extended arms," "in the lees of walls and gutters" (12, 18, 18, 62, 79, 80, 88, 174, 210, 251, 267). The reporter's travelling down so many tunnels also suggests the sexual nature of his quest for Laverne. Perhaps too they are reminiscent of the trenches of the warblasted European landscape, another kind of wasteland. Cf. Henri Barbusse, Under Fire: The Story of a Squad [New York: Dutton, 1917]: "Now you can make out a network of long ditches . . . It is the trench" (278); "lines of ruts that glisten like steel rails" (15).

11.28 vulcanised: Crude or synthetic rubber is vulcanized to make it less plastic, less sticky, and less influenced by cold and heat. The confetti is compacted and hardened. This is one of many chemical processes and synthetic products mentioned throughout Pylon. (See also notes 65.15, 192.17, 208.20-21, and 312.19, for example.)

12.2 trolley wire: The overhead electric lines along which the streetcars run, and an appropriate metaphor since electric streetcars have operated in New Orleans since 1892 (City Guide 35).

12.28 Roger Shumann: Blotner suggests that he resembles Faulkner's friend and instructor, Vernon Omlie, an expert pilot (Faulkner 866), who with his wife Phoebe started a flying school and founded Mid-South Airways in Memphis. He had taught flying during the war and later drifted into barnstorming (Faulkner 796). Faulkner began taking lessons from Omlie on February 2, 1933 (Faulkner 275). Blotner also writes, "If the young Roger Shumann resembled Carl Ericson in The Trail of the Hawk," Sinclair Lewis' 1915 novel about aviation and a Midwestern youth, "here his precocity suggested Jimmy Wedell" (Faulkner 873). Wedell was a local hero in Louisiana (as a museum dedicated to him in Patterson,

Louisiana, attests) who raced and designed planes and also started his own flying school and company for building aircraft. Blotner writes, "He was a young man who had first come to prominence at the National Air Races in Cleveland" in 1931 (<u>Faulkner</u> 834) and who won a major race the second day of the New Orleans races in his famous "45" (<u>Times-Picayune</u> 16 Feb. 1934: 1). Judith Wittenberg feels that Roger was modeled after Faulkner's younger brother Dean, who was a pilot and with his wife was "at the real center" of the flying "subculture, spending nearly all of their time in and around airports" (<u>Faulkner</u>: <u>The Transfiguration of Biography</u> [Lincoln: U of Nebraska P, 1979] 136). (See also note 220.11.) Brooks suggests that Shumann's ancestors within Faulkner's fiction are the Sartoris twins, John and Bayard, of <u>Flags in the Dust</u>. John was shot down in World War I, Bayard dying later in the crash of an experimental plane he was testing (180). Bleikasten (see note "title") suggests that Shumann is named for "<u>Shou</u>," which "dans la mythologie egyptienne, est le nom du dieu de l'air" ("<u>Pylon</u>, Ou L'enfer" 446). Both Millgate and Brooks find similarities between Roger's two accidents and actual events at the airshow (see notes 163.9-10 and 299.5).

13.1-3 a paper: one of the colored ones, the pink or green editions of the diurnal dogwatches: the pink or green front page might be in honor of either the Carnival or the air show. In publishing and printing, dogwatch, also known as lobster trick or sunrise watch, is the "shift of newspapermen after the regular editions have gone to press" (Lester V. Barrey and Melvin Van Den Bark, comps., The American Thesaurus of Slang, 2nd ed. [New York: Crowell, 1953] 246). Faulkner's choice of "diurnal," as opposed to "daily," which also would alliterate with " dogwatches," is interesting as a diurnal was, originally, a book of devotional exercises (The Compact Edition of the Oxford English Dictionary, 1971).

13.20-21 in the three-seventy-five cubic inch: Jiggs refers to engine size, the principle by which planes are grouped for the races. The power of the engine depends on the volume of fuel and air that is compressed and then burned. Specifically, the formula is that the piston surface area times the length of stroke or piston travel times the number of cylinders equals displacement. In other words, the bigger the engine, the faster the plane should fly.

14.8-9 a plump, bland, innocently sensual Levantine face: As evidence that Feinman is Shushan (see note 14.22-23), the portrait of Shushan which hangs today at Lakefront (once Shushan) Airport is of a plump, smooth- and dark-skinned man.

14.17 FEINMAN AIRPORT: In a letter to his editor Hal Smith, Faulkner says that Feinman Airport is Shushan Airport in New Orleans (Blotner, Faulkner 875). Huey Long designed Shushan "to be the largest and most modern in the world at that time," W. Adolphe Roberts writes. "It was built at an approximate cost of $3,000,000 on filled-in land and completed in 1935" (Lake Pontchartrain [New York: Bobbs-Merrill, 1946] 338). The City Guide describes Shushan as "modern in design and artistically notable" (297). This modern design integrated art, architecture, and industry in a building in the very latest of styles--Art Deco. "Naturally the industry featured was aviation, which became the overriding theme of the project" (Joan Maloney, Art and Architecture at Lakefront Airport [pamphlet in commemoration of fiftieth anniversary of Lakefront Airport, 1984] 1). "Two large hangars . . . possess ultra-modern equipment," and the main building is luxurious and decorated by murals (see notes 37.27-38.1). An octagonal, 60-foot control tower "surmounts the Administration Building and commands an unobstructed view of the lakefront and the city in the distance" (City Guide 297).

14.18 NEW VALOIS, FRANCIANA: Brooks has already pointed out that "New Valois is New Orleans and Francia [sic] is Louisiana" (400). Faulkner himself, in a letter to Smith, wrote, "New Valois is a thinly disguised (that is, someone will read the story and believe it to be) New Orleans" (Selected Letters 86-87). As to how Faulkner came up with New Valois, perhaps it is meant to suggest the original French name of the city, La Nouvelle Orléans. Valois was also a medieval county and duchy of northern France (Leon E. Seltzer, ed., The Columbia Lippincott Gazetteer of the World

[New York: Columbia UP, 1962] 2003). As for Franciana, New Orleans was founded by the French, Louisiana named for Louis XIV.

14.22-23 COLONEL H. I. FEINMAN, CHAIRMAN SEWAGE BOARD: Though Faulkner stated to Hal Smith that Feinman Airport was Shushan Airport, "named for a politian [sic]," he described Feinman as "fiction so far as I know" (Blotner, Faulkner 875). There are obvious similarities between A. L. Shushan and H. I. Feinman, and Faulkner is likely to have made this disclaimer to his editor because of the potential for a libel suit. While Shushan was president of the Levee Board, Feinman is chairman of the Sewage Board. Abraham Shushan was Jewish; Feinman is described as "Levantine" (P 14). Both men put their names everywhere in their respective airports (Roberts 338-339 and P 15). Roberts lists Shushan, who supervised the erection of the terminal Huey P. Long designed, as part of the "ring," "the more greedy and venal followers" of Long who, after his death, "partially took over the machine he had created," completing some of his unfinished works and extending others, generally grabbing "as much as they could," inventing new taxes and pocketing the proceeds, voting huge benefits for themselves, and engineering other kinds of frauds (338).

14.25-26 This airport was Raised up and Created out of the Waste Land at the bottom of Lake Rambaud: Shushan Airport

was built on "land reclaimed from Lake Pontchartrain" (City
Guide 297). The Biblical language here, "Raised up and
Created," suggests the story of God's creation of the earth
in Genesis or of Moses, who parted the Red Sea, "made the sea
dry land" (Exodus 14:21). "Waste Land" is the first of many
references to the poetry of T. S. Eliot. Finally, Lake
Rambaud is Lake Pontchartrain, if Feinman Airport is
Shushan. Perhaps Faulkner named his fictional lake after
Arthur Rimbaud (1854-1891), the French poet (whose name is,
of course, pronounced like that of Faulkner's lake).

14.27 One Million Dollars: Roberts approximated the cost of
Shushan Airport (see note 14.17) at $3,000,000 (Lake
Pontchartrain 338), but the Times-Picayune reported the cost
at $4,000,000 (10 Feb. 1934: 1).

15.21 iron balconies: The iron balconies indicate that the
bus has turned into the French Quarter. These balconies, one
of the chief distinctions of New Orleans architecture, are
made of wrought iron or cast iron and are often described as
lace-like or web-like. The wrought iron, which was
originally imported from Seville, is older, finer, and more
costly, but the locally-made cast iron depicts native plant
life like the morning glory, maize, or live oak (City Guide
148). The balconies are useful as well as beautiful,
shielding the patio and street walls against sun and rain and
providing all rooms with light and air (James M. Fitch,

"Creole Architecture 1718-1860: The Rise and Fall of a Great Tradition," Past as Prelude 79).

15.22 dirty paved courts: Like the iron balconies, these were a feature that residents of the French Quarter built into their homes "to provide comfort and spaciousness in a neighborhood which, with its sloppy, poorly drained streets and narrow lots, gave evidence of neither" (City Guide 147). Generally, a flagstone alleyway leads from the sidewalk to an inner courtyard garden, surrounded by high walls. In the twenties when Faulkner was living in New Orleans and in the thirties, the time during which Pylon is set, parts of the Quarter were decaying and run-down, as are some sections even today. The 1938 edition of the City Guide describes some buildings as "decrepit and dingy, with doors sagging and ironwork rust-eaten" while others are standing vacant and in ruins (231).

15.23 cobbled streets: The streets in the Quarter were and are brick, although some sidewalks were paved with "imported cobbles or flags" (Fitch 77).

15.24-26 low brick walls which seemed to sweat a rich slow overfecund smell of fish and coffee and sugar: New Orleans is a port city and the French Quarter, through which Jiggs is passing, is bounded by the Mississippi River. Fish is sold at the French Market on the riverfront, and there were coffee stands at either end of the Market. Both coffee and sugar were once unloaded at the riverfront wharves (City Guide 274, 281). The character Elmer, in Faulkner's uncompleted 1925 novel, has a similar experience in New Orleans, "smelling the rich smells of earth in a quick hastened fecundity, and overripeness; sugar and fruit" (Elmer, ed. Dianne Cox, Mississippi Quarterly 36[1983]: 383). In "Preludes," first collected in Prufrock and Other Observations (London: Egoist, 1917), Eliot writes of city smells, including the smell of "coffee stands" (Collected Poems: 1909-1935 [New York: Harcourt, Brace, 1936] 24).

15.26-28 and another odor profound faint and distinctive as a musty priest's robe; of some spartan effluvium of mediaeval convents: "Effluvium" is a word that Faulkner uses frequently. Asked why smell is so important in Sartoris and The Unvanquished, he responded, "I can't say unless smell is one of my sharper senses, maybe it's sharper than sight" (Faulkner in the University: Class Conferences at the University of Virginia 1957-1958, eds. Joseph Blotner and Frederick Gwyn [Charlottesville: U of Virginia P, 1959] 253). The priests appear also in Mosquitoes, though the sense emphasized is sound rather than smell. "Three gray, soft-footed priests had passed on, but in an interval hushed by windowless old walls there lingers yet a thin celibate despair"([New York: Boni & Liveright, 1927] 335). A very similar passage appears in Elmer: "Three gray soft-footed priests had passed on, but in interval hushed by windowless old walls there lingered like an odor a thin celibate despair" (419). Each of these "priest" passages is set down in stark contrast to something more worldly--to the "overfecund smell" in Pylon (15) and to Gordon's journey through the Quarter towards a brothel in the final chapter of Mosquitoes. Cf. "The Priest," New Orleans Sketches (4-5). Perhaps the influence here is Keats' "Eve of St. Agnes" with its medieval setting and ancient beadsman.

16.1 bearded liveoak groves: The live oak (Quercus virginiana) is evergreen, thus the "live." The beards are Spanish moss (see note 16.9).

16.5 cabins . . . upon stilts: Many houses along the Louisiana coast are elevated off the ground on piers "to provide better exposure to the breeze, to escape periodic flooding and invasion by vermin" (Fitch 75). What Jiggs is probably seeing are fishermen's huts characteristic of the marshes and actually built over the water on pilings (Louisiana: A Guide 159).

16.6 shell foundation of road: Oyster shells were used like gravel to surface roads along the Gulf Coast (Calvin S. Brown, A Glossary of Faulkner's South [New Haven: Yale UP, 1976] 144).

16.8 nets: For fishing and shrimping.

16.9 smokecolored growth: Spanish moss (<u>Tillandsia usneoides</u>) grows profusely in southern Louisiana, draping the cypresses and live oaks in long festoons. Though it is actually an air-feeding plant with no roots whatsoever, many people believe that Spanish moss is a parasite, feeding off a host tree and eventually destroying it. The moss is gray, and gets its color from scale-hairs through which it obtains and preserves water. "Just how it obtains enough nutrients for its subsistence is still somewhat of a mystery" (Wilhelmina F. Greene and Hugo L. Blomquist, <u>Flowers of the South</u>, <u>Native and Exotic</u> [Chapel Hill: U of North Carolina P, 1953] 146). Most of the plants and animals Faulkner mentions throughout <u>Pylon</u> have, or were believed to have, unusual, sometimes ominous, ways of adapting to their environment (see notes 17.7, 17.7, 174.26, 241.26-27, 267.21, for example).

16.28 jack: Money.

17.7 sawgrass: (<u>Cladium jamaicense</u>) A sedge of fresh and brackish marshes, the dominant species over vast areas of Louisiana marsh as late as the mid-1950s (R. H. Chabreck and R. E. Condrey, <u>Common Vascular Plants of the Louisiana Marsh</u> [Baton Rouge: LSU Center for Wetland Resources, 1979] 26). The plant has narrow leaves with sharply serrated edges, sharp enough to cut anyone trying to force his way through this grass (Brown 169). Its seeds are very durable, able to persist on the marsh floor for many years (Chabreck and Condrey 26); (see note 16.9).

17.7 cypress: The swamp or bald cypress (<u>Taxodium distichum</u>) grows to 100 to 120 feet, narrowly pyramidal in shape with buttressed roots which, in water, produce knees, woody humps the purpose of which puzzles scientists. These knees do not supply air to the roots as was thought in the past (Hugh Johnson, <u>The International Book of Trees</u> [New York: Simon and Schuster, 1973] 112-113); (see note 16.9).

17.16 pennons: Wittenberg suggests that the aura of pennons "always surrounds Faulkner's doomed horseborne heroes" (136), as the title of Faulkner's novel of horse- and air-borne heroes suggests--<u>Flags in the Dust</u>.

17.27 crenelated: An architectural term "describing a parapet in which the top is alternately and uniformly depressed," like a battlement (Henry H. Saylor, <u>Dictionary of Architecture</u> [New York: Wiley, 1952] 48).

18.5-8 miniature replicas of the concrete runways on the field itself: . . . laid by compass to all the winds: "Shushan airport's four runways were laid out to the cardinal points of the compass" (Harrison 155).

18.7,11 four Fs . . . two capital Fs: Feinman has placed his initial all over the airport as did Shushan (see notes 14.17 and 14.22-23), who "put the word 'Shushan,' or the letter 'S,' in every available spot, repeating it literally scores of times in metal and stone. Once he boasted that it would cost not less than $50,000 to remove his trademark" (Roberts 338-339). As Faulkner wrote his editor Hal Smith, "Shushan Airport has a lot of capital S's about it" like Feinman with its F's (Selected Letters 86).

18.21 braces: Suspenders.

19.8 rockerarms: A part of the valve mechanism of an engine which opens and closes the intake and exhaust valves to allow the fuel and air mixture into the cylinder and combustion products to exhaust. In an in-line engine, as opposed to a v or radial engine, the rods (see note 19.8, "rods") and rocker-arms might suggest a ribcage. (See "the halfeaten carcass of a deer," P 19 and also note 7.15-16.)

19.8 rods: Push rods are also part of the valve mechanism of an engine and transfer motion from a cam to a rocker-arm which in turn opens and closes the valves (see preceding note).

19.16 one taller: This is Jack Holmes, first identified as the taller man, then as the jumper (P 30). We are not given his full name until p. 129. Millgate has noted that, like Jack, a famous jumper named Clem Sohn performed a delayed parachute drop at the actual airshow releasing flour from a bag as he fell (see notes 27.19, 34.2); that Jack Monahan was caught in "a cross-current of wind" and blown against the seawall (139), dislocating his shoulder rather than injuring his leg (Times-Picayune 15 Feb. 1934: 3); that Eris Daniels, another jumper, was blown off course into the lake as she fell (139). Blotner's description of William Spratling's (see note 57.8) "neatly clipped dark brown mustache above a rather sensitive mouth" (Faulkner 401) is reminiscent of the description of Jack: "He wore a narrow moustache above a mouth much more delicate and even feminine than that of the woman who he and Jiggs called Laverne" (P 34). A caricature of Spratling is included in his and Faulkner's Sherwood Anderson & Other Famous Creoles (1926) (Austin: U of Texas P, 1966). The critics have almost nothing to say about Jack or his ancestry in Faulkner's fiction. In his rigidity and potential for violence he seems, to me, most like Jewel Bundren. Brooks does include both him and Roger in a discussion of Faulkner's attitude toward fighter pilots and aerial acrobats, asserting that Faulkner did not see them as "gay cavaliers," but that he does not "deny Shumann and Holmes courage, and a sense of honor" (403).

19.24 Laverne: Laverne's name, of course, suggests spring (see note 22.16-17). Blotner feels that her character "owed

a good deal to Phoebe Fairgrave Omlie" (Faulkner 866), wife
of Vernon Omlie (see note 12.28), a tiny woman with "hair
cropped like a man's" whom he met in Minneapolis and taught
to wingwalk (Faulkner 796). As Millgate points out, the
participation of Eris Daniels, the only woman, in "the
jumping event suggests a possible source for certain aspects
of Faulkner's presentation of Laverne" (138; Times-Picayune
17 Feb. 1934: 1). Many critics have commented upon Laverne's
ancestry within Faulkner's fiction. Millgate compares her to
Lena Grove of Light in August and Eula Varner of The Hamlet:
"they are 'earth-mother' figures, symbols of continuity,
permanence, and rebirth, and it may not be an accident that
the names of the three women are near-anagrams of each other"
(142). Brooks finds her harder to place: "She doesn't really
fit with the 'masculinized' women such as Drusilla Hawk
Sartoris or Joanna Burden," "lacks the coyness and the
coquettish manipulation of men" of Cecily Saunders and Temple
Drake, has nothing other than a kind of ruthlessness in
common with Narcissa Benbow, but is closest to Charlotte
Rittenmeyer, both ruthless with themselves and others, living
without "reference to the future," though Charlotte has her
all-consuming dream which Laverne does not have (400).

20.25-28 something which had apparently crept from a doctor's
cupboard and, in the snatched garments of an etherised
patient in a charity ward, escaped into the living world: A
famous German silent film, released in 1919, "The Cabinet of

Doctor Caligari," is the story of a hypnotist who oversees a mental hospital and forces his slave, Cesare, his face white with paint, to leave the coffin-like cupboard where he is kept and supposedly commit murder (Gerald Mast, A Short History of the Movies, 3rd ed. [Indianapolis: Bobbs-Merrill, 1981] 131-132).

20.26 etherised patient in a charity ward: Cf. "The Love Song of J. Alfred Prufrock," T. S. Eliot, which first appeared in Prufrock and Other Observations, 1917: "When the evening is spread out against the sky/ Like a patient etherised upon a table" (Collected Poems 11). Cf. "Portrait of Elmer," "beneath a sky like a patient etherised and dying after an operation" (Uncollected Stories of William Faulkner, ed. Joseph Blotner [New York: Random House, 1979] 623).

21.2 doped: Fabric wings were made taut, air-tight, and waterproof through treatment with cellulose nitrate or acetate, known as dope (see note 78.20).

21.11 Dempsey: William H. "Jack" Dempsey (1895-1983), an American boxer who defended his title successfully five times before losing it in 1926 to Gene Tunney (New York Times Biographical Service 12[1983]: 661).

21.11-12 How about taking me on for an icecream cone?: Quentin buys the little Italian girl an ice cream cone in The

Sound and the Fury. "How about some ice cream?" he asks her ([New York: Jonathan Cape and Harrison Smith, 1929] 158).

22.4 unbonneted: The bonnet is the engine cover or hood.

22.5 supercharger: A compressor or blower device for increasing the amount of air available for the combustion process (the engine runs on a mixture of air and fuel), thus increasing the engine's power. As an aircraft climbs, the amount of mixture drawn into the engine is reduced because of reduced atmospheric pressure; thus less power is available. The supercharger provides more power without increasing the weight of the engine.

22.12 crescent wrench: An adjustable wrench for turning bolt heads and nuts. Crescent is a trade name that became generic.

22.16-17 the mealcolored, the strong pallid Iowacorncolored, hair: The references here to meal and corn not only describe Laverne's blond hair, but also connect her with Demeter and her daughter Persephone whom J. G. Frazer identifies as "goddesses of the corn" (The Golden Bough: A Study in Magic and Religion [New York: MacMillan, 1922] 396). Joan Serafin identifies Demeter more broadly as the "goddess of agriculture, productive soil, fruitfulness of mankind, and guardian of marriage" (Faulkner's Uses of the Classics [Ann

Arbor: UMI Research, 1983] 159). Traditionally, Demeter's hair is described as golden.

22.24 cowling: Another term for engine cover or hood.

22.25 set the propeller horizontal: In order to clear the ground when the plane is lifted by its tail and, in this case, walked through the hangar door.

22.30 apron: The extensive paved surface located in front of the entrance of the hangar and used for loading, unloading, parking, and repairing airplanes.

23.2 reporter: According to Brooks, the reporter can not be precisely associated with any real-life person, yet "one or two details may have been derived from the veteran reporter on the New Orleans Item, Hermann Deutsch," whose by-line appeared on several stories about the 1934 airshow (399). Brooks, who met Deutsch in the thirties, was reminded of him upon reading Pylon by the reporter's height, thinness, but most of all by "his shambling gait" (399; also conversation with Professor Brooks, University of South Carolina, May, 1984). When Brooks asked Deutsch if the reporter were modeled after him, he answered that he might have been "only in the sense that he was with Faulkner at the airport a good deal during the air carnival and that Faulkner might well have seen him walking about with a little boy belonging to

one of the aviators riding on his shoulders" (399). As for
the reporter's namelessness, Faulkner told an audience at
Nagano in 1955: "I have written about characters whose names
I never did know. Because they didn't tell me. There was
one in Pylon, for instance, he was the central character in
the book, he never did tell me who he was. I don't know
until now what his name was. That was the reporter, he was a
protagonist" (Lion in the Garden 131-132). Critics have
speculated about his name. Helen Barthelme in her 1976
dissertation guesses Lazarus ("Pylon The Doomed Quest. A
Critical and Textual Study of William Faulkner's Neglected
Allegory," U of Texas at Austin). More recently, Peter
Jordan has proposed J. Alfred Prufrock as the reporter's
name ("April Fool!" Notes on Mississippi Writers 12[1979]:
17-22). These are interesting suggestions, but I do not
think that Faulkner ever intended the reporter to have a
name. Brooks feels that the reporter's ancestors in
Faulkner's fiction are Horace Benbow and Gavin Stevens, both
"idealistic romantics" unable to understand womankind.
"Faulkner evidently felt a compulsion to explore the
encounter, usually comic but sometimes tragic, in which the
idealist comes up against unyielding actuality" (195). Louis
Berman's description of the "thyroid personality" sounds as
if it were written specifically about the reporter: "During
maturity, the type are characterized usually by a lean body,
or a tendency rapidly to become thin under stress. . . .
Sexually they are well differentiated and susceptible.

Noticeable emotivity, a rapidity of perception and volition, and a tendency to explosive crises of expression are the distinctive psychic traits. A restless, inexhaustable energy makes them perpetual doers and workers, who get up early in the morning, flit about all day, retire late, and frequently suffer from insomnia" (The Glands Regulating Personality: A Study of the Glands of Secretion in Relation to the Types of Human Nature [New York: MacMillan, 1922] 216-217). Though he does not mention Pylon specifically, Mick Gidley finds evidence in Faulkner's work that he knew this book ("Another Psychologist, a Physiologist and William Faulkner," Ariel 2[1971]: 78-86). Also, according to Blotner, Phil Stone ordered or purchased Berman's book in April of 1922 (William Faulkner's Library--A Catalog [Charlottesville: UP of Virginia, 1964] 123). A summary of Freud's theory of the id also sounds strikingly like the reporter: "It wants immediate gratification. It is demanding, impulsive, irrational, asocial, selfish, and pleasure loving . . . . The id does not think. It only rushes into action" (Calvin S. Hall, A Primer of Freudian Psychology [New York: New American Library, 1954] 27).

23.21 amplifier: In the galley proofs this is spelled "amplifyer." A proofreader has Americanized the spelling throughout; Faulkner has okayed the correction (see note 7.18).

23.25 skeleton: Gustave Doré's illustrations of Don Quixote (see note 49.15) show a skeletal man. Faulkner's copy of the 1930 Modern Library edition of the novel, John Ozell's revision of the translation of Peter Motteux, which includes these illustrations, is inscribed "20 Oct. 1938," three years after the publication of Pylon (Blotner, Catalog 102). Yet these are famous illustrations, completed by Doré in 1863 as part of his series of illustrated classics. Faulkner certainly could have seen them in another edition of Quixote before 1934; for example the Hogarth Press of New York used these illustrations in their 1900 edition of Don Quixote.

24.2 circuitriderlooking: A circuit rider is a "preacher who makes a regular circuit of country churches, preaching at a different one each Sunday" (Brown 53). According to Harrison, this character, later identified as Bob Bullitt, was based on Steve Wittman, "premier air racer and experimental aeroplane designer.... Wittman, a slender, lantern-jawed man whose wire-rimmed spectacles give him a markedly clerical appearance," participated in the New Orleans air races, setting a world class record (156).

24.3 Graves Trophy race: Wittman (see note 24.2) won the Greve Trophy at the All-American air meet in Miami, in December of 1935 (Harrison 157); (see note 31.6-7).

24.16-18 a woman not tall and not thin, looking almost like a man in the greasy coverall: Cf. "Raid" and The Unvanquished. Drusilla "was not tall; it was the way she stood and walked. She had on pants, like a man" (Saturday Evening Post 3 Nov. 1934; [New York: Random House, 1938] 103). Cf. The Wild Palms Charlotte's "got on pants . . . . man's pants" ([New York: Random House, 1939] 6).

24.18 ragged hair: Cf. Elmer: "Jo's straight black hair. . . was hacked raggedly, as though she would not remain still long enough to have it properly trimmed." Later Elmer describes his sister's hair as a "cracked and jagged bell" (Mississippi Quarterly 36[1983]: 354, 351). Cf. "Raid" and The Unvanquished, where Drusilla's "hair was short; it looked like Father's would when he would tell Granny about him and the men cutting each other's hair with a bayonet" (103).

24.19-20 a tanned heavy-jawed face: Charlotte Rittenmeyer is also described, by the doctor whom Harry fetches to treat her, as having a "heavy jaw" (The Wild Palms). Pat's jaw "in profile was heavy: there was something masculine about it" (Mosquitoes 23-24). Brooks cites Faulkner's description of Helen Baird in an undated letter: "I remember a sullen-jawed yellow-eyed belligerent gal" (52).

24.30 cheap metal vanity: A woman's compact with a mirror.

25.12-17 Then she turned her back slightly toward the door and in the same motion with which she reached for the skirt she stepped out of the coverall in a pair of brown walking shoes . . . and a man's thin cotton undershorts and nothing else. Cf. Elmer: Elmer watches his sister as "her angling arms drag her dress over her head . . . . Jo wore beneath her dress a man's sleeveless undershirt . . . and a funny nether garment she had made herself from coarse cloth, so that she resembled a small boy in his larger brother's short pants" (351). Cf. Sanctuary: "Temple sprang to her feet. She unfastened her dress, her arms arched thin and high, her shadow anticking her movements. In a single motion she was out of it, crouching a little, match-thin in her scant undergarments" ([New York: Modern Library, 1932] 82).

25.18 starting bomb: Indicates what Harrison describes as a "racehorse" start. At the sound of a bomb, all the planes took off, "proceeded to a special scattering pylon, and then entered the triangular course" (157).

26.8 zoomed: The "simplest of all aerobatic manoeuvres"; from level flight, the plane suddenly climbs upward at a steep angle (Harrison 12).

27.3 Mardi Gras: Mardi Gras (Fat Tuesday) is the last day of Carnival (farwell to the flesh) and the day before Ash Wednesday and Lent. However, the term is often used by locals to refer to the entire Carnival, which is celebrated by street masking and parades and masked balls organized by secret krewes. The nature of the celebration is both pagan and Christian, "rooted in the pre-Christian celebrations of the advent of spring, rescued from their maelstrom of pagan debauchery, cleansed into Christian rite, and transmitted into the feast of the flesh before the fasting commemorating Christ's fast, the period of revelry which the volatile Latins of Italy, France and Spain required before the forty days of Lent (excluding Sundays) preceding Easter" (Goreau 342-343). Mardi Gras has been known to Louisiana since Iberville took possession of the country in 1699 (City Guide 175).

27.10 THURSDAY (DEDICATION DAY): The actual dedication ceremony for Shushan Airport was held on Friday afternoon, February 9, 1934 (Millgate 139); then, because of rain, the show and races were postponed until the day after Mardi Gras, Ash Wednesday, February 14 and ran through February 17 (Brooks 395). For a complete discussion of the chronology of Pylon as compared to the actual events of the dedication of the airport and the airshow, see Brooks' appendices in Toward Yoknapatawpha, 395-396.

27.11 Spot Parachute Jump: Jumping with the intention of landing in a specified spot, hitting a target; an event included in the actual airshow (Times-Picayune 15 Feb. 1934:

3), February 15, the day Faulkner arrived (Blotner, _Faulkner_ 833). A chute man was a standard member of any barnstorming team like that made up of Roger, Jack, Laverne, and Jiggs; and the spot and delayed jumps were standard events in any airshow. Though Leonardo da Vinci had conceived of parachutes centuries before, they were not used even in WWI, except at the very end of the war in a limited way. Though between the World Wars parachutes were improved, skydiving in the thirties was still new, risky, and thus thrilling for a crowd at an airshow.

27.12 Dash: These races at Feinman Airport are closed-circuit as opposed to cross-country, point to point. Closed-circuit racing consists of several laps at low altitude and relatively high speed around a course marked by pylons. Planes compete singly or at intervals for lowest elapsed time or as a group, as is the case in _Pylon_, the winner being the first to complete the course.

27.15 Aerial Acrobatics: The performance of stunts such as dives, loops, steep banks, and rolls in an aircraft were a feature of the actual airshow at Shushan. Roy Hunt and Art Davis exhibited sky writing, "dog fights," and aerobatics or aerial acrobatics (_Times_-_Picayune_ 16 Feb. 1934: 1, 2) (see note 60.6-7).

27.17 Scull Dash: Shell Oil Company sponsored a timed race over a straight course--the Shell Speed Dash (Harrison 157).

27.19 Delayed Parachute Drop: The jumper delays opening his parachute until he is apparently dangerously close to the ground. The Times-Picayune for February 14, 1934, announced that "Clem Sohn, world's champion delayed parachute jumper, will bail out at 10,000 feet and fall free to within 300 feet of the ground" (1, 16). The ripcord parachute, which allowed free-fall, was not invented until 1918 and was first used for an emergency in 1922 (Herbert S. Zim, Parachutes [New York: Harcourt, Brace, 1942] 29). Even into the thirties many argued that the attached-type, automatic chutes--which, because the ripcord was attached to the plane itself, opened automatically when the jumper leapt from the plane--were safer (Zim 29). The belief that a jumper might black out during his long fall and fail to pull the ripcord died hard. More than likely, many of the spectators would have been unfamiliar with a parachute the jumper himself could open as he fell. For a few moments at least, then, the crowd might imagine that the man jumped to certain death (Harrison 158).

27.20-21 Rocket Plane: Usually an airplane using a rocket or rockets for its chief or only propulsion, but here Faulkner probably refers to W. Merle Nelson of Los Angeles, a noted stunt flyer of the time, who displayed "loops and other spectacular maneuvers . . . by means of rockets, which

discharged a continuous stream of fire from the plane"
(<u>Times</u>-<u>Picayune</u> 15 Feb. 1934: 1).

27.21 Lieut. Frank Burnham: W. Merle Nelson (see preceding
note).

28.3 scarecrow: Cf. "Men are just accumulations dolls stuffed
with sawdust swept up from the trash heaps where all previous
dolls had been thrown away the sawdust flowing from what
wound in what side that not for me died not" (<u>The Sound and
the Fury</u> 218). Cf. "We are the stuffed men/ leaning
together/ Headpiece filled with straw. Alas!" (T. S.
Eliot, "The Hollow Men," <u>Dial</u> 78[1925]; <u>Collected Poems</u>
101).

28.17-18 perfectly grave: Lena Grove is often described as
grave. Cf. "Lena's lowered face is grave, quiet" (<u>Light in
August</u> [New York: Harrison Smith and Robert Haas, 1932] 18).

29.21-24 the scarecrow man . . . the small khaki spot of the
little boy's dungarees riding high on his shoulder: (See note
23.2.)

30.12-13 reclaimed and tortured earth: Shushan Airport was
built on filled-in land (see note 14.25-26). First a
retaining wall was built, outlining the land mass they wanted
to create, a dead reef of oyster shells piled up on either

side of it. Then the area inside the wall was built up with hydraulic fill, which means that the lake bottom was dredged then pumped up into the walled-in area.

31.6-7 Graves Trophy . . . in Miami in December: In 1929 Miami's municipal airfield inaugurated an annual airshow, eventually called the Miami All-American Air Maneuvers. They held their show in the dead of winter when other shows were unable to operate, and they attracted "the nation's best stunt pilots and racers as well as a large contingent of military airplanes" (Paul O'Neil, Barnstormers and Speed Kings [Alexandria, VA: Time-Life Books, 1981] 25). Though the Graves Trophy is fictional (see note 24.3) the Schneider, Pulitzer, Thompson, and Bendix Trophies were the prizes in four major air races.

31.8 Chance Specials: Special because most racing airplanes were "designed, built, flown, and named by their owners" (Harrison 157) (see note 47.27).

31.9-10 Vas you dere, Sharlie?: A line made famous by Baron Munchausen, a radio comedian of the 1930s (Joseph Blotner, "Notes for Pylon," William Faulkner: Novels 1930-1935 [New York: Library of America, 1985] 1033).

31.19 the voice was firm: Harrison identifies Faulkner's original here as Jack Storey, "the wisecracking master of ceremonies of the Pan-American meet" (158).

31.26 modest winged badge: According to Blotner, Faulkner occasionally wore such a badge, indicating his membership in Quiet Birdmen (1033); (see note 61.2).

32.3 Yair; he'd make lard, now: The man is fat. Cf. I Henry IV II.ii where "Falstaff sweats to death and lards the lean earth" (William Shakespeare: The Complete Works [Baltimore: Penguin, 1969] 680). Lard bucket, tub of lard, or lard-ass are the more common versions of this insult.

32.11 dope: Slang for information, in this case, the predictions about who would win the race which the flyers fed to the announcer.

33.25 Lazarus: Jesus raised Lazarus from the dead. Cf. John 11:38-44. Cf. Luke 16:19-31: Lazarus is not allowed to return from the dead to testify to the rich man's brothers. Cf. "The Love Song of J. Alfred Prufrock," T. S. Eliot: "I am Lazarus, come from the dead" (Collected Poems 15).

34.2 sack: A sack of flour. The jumper would leave a stream of flour as he fell through the sky, making him easier to spot as he fell from a high altitude and dramatizing the distance of this free-fall (see note 27.19). Clem Sohn (see note 19.16) used a sack of flour for his jump at the airshow at Shushan (Millgate 13).

35.21 emergency parachute: A reserve parachute which the jumper wears in case the main chute fails to open. The main chute is worn on the back, the emergency chute on the front of the body.

35.22 Yair, we're jake now: Jake is slang for all right.

36.5 Should be about dead up there now: There are no drafts to blow the jumper off his course. Landing in the lake would be treacherous, the weight of the sodden parachute pulling him under and causing him to drown.

37.14-15 fall for almost four miles before pulling the ripcord: This must be an exaggeration. Clem Sohn (see note 27.19) was scheduled to make a 10,000-foot jump at the airshow (Times-Picayune 15 Feb. 1934: 3) and actually dropped "nearly two miles" before opening his chute (Times-Picayune 16 Feb. 1934: 1). It was not until 1940 that Arthur Starnes made a delayed jump from 30,800 feet, and he jumped not to set a record but as an experiment to "discover the effects of high altitude delayed jumps on the parachutist" (Zim 111). Before Starnes made this jump safely, many believed that delayed jumping from such altitudes was much too risky, if not impossible.

37.17-19 breasting now with immobility the comparatively thin tide which still set toward the apron: Though more often it is the confetti and serpentine which drift and rain (see note 7.2), the crowds are also described in terms of water, as here and later--"A steady stream of people flowed along the concrete gutters" (P 140). Crowds which move like water are also a repeated image in Sherwood Anderson's Poor White: "Hugh looked at the people who were whirled along past him"; "the rush of people began again . . . in waves as water washes along a beach during a storm" ([New York: Huebsch, 1920] 31). Cf. "The Waste Land," T. S. Eliot: "A crowd flowed over London Bridge . . . Flowed up the hill and down King William Street" ([New York: Boni & Liveright, 1922]; Collected Poems 71).

37.27 relief: A large sculptural frieze chronicling the development of the airplane and the steps in its assembly circled the top of the waiting room at Shushan (Maloney 1).

37.28 bronze or chromium: The stairway and mezzanine balcony rails at Shushan were chromium and bronze and carried through the industrial, aviation theme (Maloney 1).

37.28-38.1 murallimning . . . legendary tale of what man has come to call his conquering of the infinite and impervious air: Not the murals referred to in the City Guide (see note 14.17) which are described as eight murals "On the mezzanine floor depicting early New Orleans history . . . executed by Xavier Gonzalez" (297). These historical murals actually decorated the lunch room, which adjoined the waiting room and were painted by A. J. Drysdale (Maloney 2). Eight murals by Gonzalez did decorate the mezzanine, and Faulkner describes their content accurately. "The murals depict eight different sections of the world with the arrival of the airplane as their unifying factor"--Egypt, Paris, Rio de Janeiro, Bali, Mount Everest, and New York (Maloney 1). The real focal point of each of the murals I have seen and those reproduced in the commemorative pamphlet is a huge manmade monument like an Egyptian or Hindu temple, a Mayan pyramid, the Eiffel Tower, or the Brooklyn Bridge, which dwarfs the airplanes included in the paintings.

40.4 dot-dot-dash-dot: F for Feinman (see note 14.22-23).

40.16 the editor: Blotner has noted that the reporter's editor, who we later learn is named Hagood (P 62), resembles Roark Bradford, "a big-faced, balding man with a thickening waistline who still had something of the country boy about him," who worked the city desk of the Times-Picayune at night in 1925 when Faulkner was living in New Orleans (Faulkner 870, 394). A caricature of Bradford is included in Sherwood Anderson & Other Famous Creoles.

41.9 yellow copy paper: The cheap, yellow newsprint upon which news stories are typed before they are set in type. Faulkner wrote for the Times-Picayune as a free-lance contributor while he was in New Orleans (see note 57.8). For his newspaper sketches he would "buy yellow copy paper over on Canal Street . . . bringing back ten cents' worth each time" (Blotner, Faulkner 411).

41.12-13 ALITY OF: Headlines and parts of headlines, along with programs and official notices, are interspersed throughout Pylon, set in bold type and all caps, italicized or blocked off, a technique also found in Joyce's Ulysses (Little Review, 1918-1920) and Dos Passos' Manhattan Transfer.

41.15 galloping consumption: Consumption is an old-fashioned term for tuberculosis of the lungs, descriptive of the wasting effect of the disease. Galloping, when used to describe any disease, means powerful and rapid.

41.21-22 sprang full-grown: Minerva, the goddess of wisdom, sprang full-grown and fully-armed from the head of her father Jupiter (Thomas Bulfinch, Bulfinch's Mythology [New York: Crowell, 1913] 7).

42.4-5 a girl in a Barricade Street crib: A prostitute. Faulkner probably refers to Rampart Steet, named after the ramparts which extended from Fort St. Jean to Fort Bourgogne (_City Guide_ 300) and one of the boundaries of the original French Quarter. During the 19th century the young men of New Orleans maintained their quadroon and octoroon mistresses in houses along the ramparts (_City Guide_ 214). Later, Rampart Street became part of the red light district where, until 1917, prostitution was legal (_City Guide_ 215, 219). Though prostitution was finally prohibited, it persisted, simply spreading to new quarters. A crib, during the era of legal prostitution, was the lowest in a hierarchy of establishments, a tiny cell, "about seven feet wide and ten feet deep, containing a bed and a chair, with one door that opened onto the street" (Phil Johnson, "Good Time Town," Carter, _Past as Prelude_ 242).

42.11 PILOT BURNED ALIVE: Millgate notes the striking similarity between the "crash of Lieut. Frank Burnham's rocket plane in _Pylon_ [see note 27.20-21] and the actual crash of Captain W. Merle Nelson, who was burned to death in the evening of the opening day of the Shushan meet 'when his small comet plane crashed to earth and was destroyed by fire'" (Millgate 140; _Times-Picayune_ 15 Feb. 1934: 1, 3). Some speculated that, blinded by the fireworks attached to his small plane, he did not realize he was so close to the ground (_Times-Picayune_ 15 Feb. 1934: 3).

42.13 city editor: Assigns and edits city rather than national news stories.

43.14 Styx: Charon ferried the dead across this river of Hades.

43.20 running my ass ragged: Here meaning that the editor had exhausted the reporter by sending him all over the city looking for news.

44.3 like the haunt of Yuletide: Like the ghost of Christmas in Dickens' A Christmas Carol (1843).

44.14 crate: An outdated or rundown airplane.

44.20 cotter keys: These look like hair pins and are passed through holes in shafts, bolts, and nuts to hold them in place.

44.23 Harlow-colored hair: Jean Harlow (1911-1937) was an American actress, a platinum blonde, who became one of the most popular stars of the thirties with her first starring role in "Hell's Angels" (1930), Howard Hughes' film about WWI flyers. Though she generally received bad reviews for her early films, "the coarse, flashy, whorish sexpot underwent a transformation into a subtle actress with a natural flair for comedy" when she switched to MGM in 1932 (Ephraim Katz, The Film Encyclopedia [New York: Crowell, 1979] 534).

44.30 before they had airmail: Once planes started crossing the country regularly, beginning in 1921 (Harrison 159) flying the mail, barnstormers had trouble making a living among people accustomed to seeing airplanes.

45.3-4 one of those Jennies the army used to sell them for cancelled stamps: A Jenny is a JN-4D, 10,000 of which were manufactured by Glenn Curtiss for WWI and just after. Thousands of these planes became available at low prices after the War (O'Neil 25). "America's principal civilian aircraft of the early 1920s," the Jenny was a biplane with thin wings braced by wooden struts "and meticulously rigged with a maze of turnbuckled wires." It was powered by an OX-5 engine (O'Neil 26).

45.9 taught her to jump parachutes: As people in rural areas became more and more accustomed to seeing airplanes flying over, the barnstormers could no longer make a living by just offering rides. One of the tactics they used to draw crowds, besides developing spectacular stunts, was to recruit "young women daredevils to increase the lure and heighten the excitement" (O'Neil 6).

47.7 vertical bank: Banking into the turn around the pylon at a 70 to 90 degree angle, which means the plane looks as if it is pivoting upon one of its wingtips.

47.13 fabric trembling: (See notes 21.2 and 78.20.)

47.27 Vic Chance: Harrison identifies Chance as Art Chester, who built the Chester Special and won the 375 cu. in. event at Shushan (160). Another source for the name might be Chance Vought, a manufacturer of aircraft until his death in 1930, known for his singular devotion to the improvement of airplanes (Anthony Robinson, ed., The Encyclopedia of American Aircraft [New York: Galahad, 1979] 396-397).

48.1 copped with: Slang for won with.

48.2 flying on commission: Shumann does not own the plane he is flying; rather, the plane's owner allows him to fly the plane in exchange for a percentage of the winnings.

48.7 mike guy: The announcer at the microphone.

48.18-19 walk the earth with your arm crooked over your head: Clearly the image describes someone protecting his head from the blackjack (see note 48.20). But it is also reminiscent of the way a baby flings its arms up around its head when it sleeps, and the passage does begin with "birthpangs to rise up out of and walk." Cf. <u>Sanctuary</u>, where Faulkner describes Ruby's baby twice with "one thin arm, upflung" as it "lay curl-palmed beside its cheek" (73). Horace Benbow looks down at the child, "its hands upflung beside its head, as though it had died in the presence of an unbearable agony which had not had time to touch it" (192).

48.20 blackjack: A small club made of a leather bag filled with shot or some other substance and used as a weapon.

48.25 immaculate conceptions: Refers to Mary's being conceived without original sin so that she would be a suitable mother for the son of God.

49.1 J. P.: Justice of the peace. Roger and Laverne were married in a civil rather than a religious ceremony.

49.5 Don Quixote: The main character in <u>Don Quixote</u> by Miguel de Saavedra Cervantes (1547-1616), the Spanish author of novels, plays, and tales. Don Quixote, having read many romances of chivalry, dresses himself in rusty armor and a cardboard helmet and sets out to travel the world righting wrongs with the aid of his squire Sancho Panza. He fights injustice in the name of a peasant girl whom he idealizes and calls Dulcinea, but Don Quixote's good intentions inevitably result in disaster, both for himself and those he seeks to help. Faulkner several times cited <u>Don Quixote</u> as one of his favorites: "Every year I read <u>Don Quixote</u>, the Bible, an hour of Dickens, <u>The Brothers Karamazov</u>, Chekov" (<u>Lion in the Garden</u> 284). (See notes 23.2, 23.25, and 216.25-29.)

50.3-4 like a Halloween mask on a boy's stick being slowly withdrawn: Cf. <u>Sanctuary</u>: "It was like a small, dead-colored mask drawn past her on a string and then away" (123).

50.19 no Lewises or Hemingways or even Tchekovs: Sinclair Lewis (1885-1951), American novelist, won the Nobel Prize for Literature, 1930. Ernest Hemingway (1899-1961), American novelist. Anton Pavlovich Chekhov (1860-1904), Russian dramatist and short-story writer. Faulkner particularly admired his fiction and described him as a short story writer of the "first water" (<u>Faulkner in the University</u> 48).

52.11 dollar watch: "A large, sturdy, open-faced nickel-plated pocket watch. There are several makes of them, and for years the standard price was one dollar" (Brown 72).

52.23 cob pipe: A pipe made from a hollowed-out, shelled end-piece of a corn cob.

53.22-23 floats, bearing grimacing and antic mimes: Each Carnival parade is sponsored by a secret organization known as a krewe, which selects a theme for its parade each year-- historical, legendary, mythological. The floats, at least in

Faulkner's time, were made primarily of papier-mâché and represented attemps to reproduce "fantasy in lumber, cloth, paint, paste, and gilt. In designing floats, proportion and perspective are distorted. The floats are built on wheeled flat carts about twenty feet long and eight feet wide. The floats can measure no more than twenty-four feet in length and nine feet in width, in order that corners may be turned with ease; and only eighteen feet in height, because of telegraph and telephone wires. Space for the men on the floats must be taken into consideration, and so, with these limitations, the figures are made grotesque in order to achieve an illusion of hugeness" (City Guide 176). These floats were and still are painted with bright colors, more intense at night "in keeping . . . with artificial light," and hung with a shimmering, tinsel-like material (City Guide 176). Mimes are maskers who ride on the floats and toss cheap trinkets to the crowd.

53.23-25 contemplated by static curbmass of amazed confettifaces, passed as though through steady rain: Cf. "In a Station of the Metro," Ezra Pound: "The apparition of these faces in the crowd;/ Petals on a wet, black bough" (Lustra [New York: Knopf, 1917]; Selected Poems [New York: New Directions, 1957] 35). Faulkner experiments with this image first in "Nocturne" in Vision in Spring (1921). The "stars" are like "confetti blown"; "And faces like shattering petals

faintly whirl before him" ([Austin: U of Texas P, 1984] 22).
(See also notes 7.2 and 7.3.)

53.25-27 walked . . . with a kind of loose and purposeless
celerity: (See note 23.2.)

54.26-27 When he reached Grandlieu Street he discovered that
the only way he could cross it would be by air: Another clue
that this is Canal Street (see note 11.19), since most
Carnival parades travel both sides of New Orleans' main
street.

55.4-8 a gust of screaming newsboys . . . as birds . . .
They swirled about him, screaming: Cf. The Sound of the Fury.
Quentin describes two bootblacks as "shrill and raucous, like
blackbirds" (102).

55.15 Boinum Boins!: Many natives of New Orleans do not speak
with a Southern accent, rather with an accent that resembles
that of certain New Yorkers. A quotation from A. J.
Liebling, "The Earl of Louisiana," included as a preface to
John Kennedy Toole's A Confederacy of Dunces, describes it
best: "There is a New Orleans city accent . . . associated
with downtown New Orleans, particularly with the German and
Irish Third Ward, that is hard to distinguish from the accent
of Hoboken, Jersey City, and Astoria, Long Island, where the
Al Smith inflection, extinct in Manhattan, has taken refuge.

The reason, as you might expect, is that the same stocks that brought the accent to Manhattan imposed it on New Orleans" (Baton Rouge: Louisiana State UP, 1980). The newsboys are shouting "Burnham Burns!" (see note 42.11).

55.26 window dummies: Slang for mannekins.

56.17-18 the smoky glare of the passing torches: During the night parades of Carnival, "dancing Negroes carry torches," or "flambeaux" (City Guide 179).

56.20-22 they resembled the tall and the short man of the orthodox and unfailing comic team: Don Quixote and Sancho Panza (see note 49.5). Mutt and Jeff, Bud Fisher's two losers upon whom fortune seems to have turned her back. Mutt, the gambler, is tall and thin, and Jeff, whom Mutt rescued from an insane asylum, is very short. This comic strip, begun in 1907, was still running in the thirties; and in 1930 Walter Lanz produced Mutt and Jeff cartoon shorts (Robinson 44). Cf. War Birds: Diary of an Unknown Aviator (1926), [Elliot White Springs]: Springs and Oliver are "the tin woodman and scarecrow from the land of Oz and they are looking for Dorothy to put them together again" ([London: Temple Press, 1966] 138). The reporter is often described as a scarecrow (see note 28.3), Jiggs a mechanical creature.

57.3-4 Moddy Graw: Jiggs' pronunciation is close to that of the newsboys, presumably natives (see note 55.15).

57.8 French town: Downtown, the French Quarter, or the Vieux Carré, meaning old square. This oldest section of the city, originally occupied primarily by French-speaking people, is bounded on the south by Canal Street, on the north by Esplanade, on the west by North Rampart, and on the east by the Mississippi River (City Guide 230). This is the section of the city where the crumbling or plastered brick buildings with iron balconies and courtyards sit almost on the narrow streets. The City Guide describes the ambiance: "The visitor will find in the French Quarter a strange and fascinating jumble of antique shops, flop houses, tearooms, wealthy homes, bars, art studios, night clubs, grocery stores, beautifully furnished apartments, and dilapidated flats." And he will meet "debutantes, artists, gamblers, drunks, streetwalkers, icemen, sailors, bank presidents, and beggars" (221). Faulkner lived in the French Quarter between January and June of 1925, first with Sherwood and Elizabeth Anderson on St. Peter Street in the Pontalba, then with William Spratling at 624 Orleans (later Pirate's) Alley (Blotner, Faulkner 388, 401).

57.26 Laughing Boy: A Pulitzer Prize-winning novel by Oliver LaFarge, an acquaintance of Faulkner's in New Orleans who is caricatured in Sherwood Anderson & Other Famous Creoles. His

1929 novel is the highly romantic story of an American Indian silversmith and horse trader; like Pylon, it involves a ménage à trois.

57.26 Woishndon Poik: Washington Park (see note 55.15).

54.20 towheaded: Having white-blond hair; tow as in the fiber of flax.

58.16-17 Hotel Terrebone: Spelled "Terrebonne" earlier (P 65), this is French for good earth. Faulkner may have named this hotel after Terrebonne bayou and parish, where the land was fertile, the bayou rich for fishing and trapping. According to Brooks, "The Terrebonne Hotel may very well be the Monteleone Hotel, in the Quarter" (401).

58.22-23 tiered identical cubicles of one thousand rented sleepings: A flop house with bunk beds, perhaps. Cf. "Preludes," T. S. Eliot: "With the other masquerades/ That time resumes,/ One thinks of all the hands/ That are raising dingy shades/ In a thousand furnished rooms" (Collected Poems 24).

58.26 Teared Q Pickles: Jiggs garbles the reporter's "tiered cubicles" (see preceding note).

58.27 rented . . . . .: The ellipses here stand for "cunts". In the galley proofs Faulkner has crossed through "sleepings" and noted in the margin--"A period for each letter in 'cunts'."

59.6 snappy: Neat, smart, attractive (Harold Wentworth and Stuart Flexner, comps., Dictionary of American Slang [New York: Crowell, 1975] 494).

60.4 Matt Ord: Jimmy Wedell held such a record (see note 12.28). The name seems closer, however, to Matty Laird, "builder of the Solution and Super Solution, two of the most successful closed-circuit race planes of the early 1930s" (Harrison 160).

60.6-7 AL MYERS. CALEXCO/ JIMMY OTT. CALEXCO: Roy Hunt and Art Davis (see note 27.15) were pilots for Texaco (Harrison 160).

60.11 (i n r i): Iesus Nazarenus, Rex Iudaeorum, Jesus of Nazareth, King of the Jews. Cf. John 19:19, "And Pilate wrote a title, and put it on the cross. And the writing was, JESUS OF NAZARETH THE KING OF THE JEWS."

60.24 lysol: Lysol, a brand of antiseptic cleanser with a powerful odor.

61.2 Q. B.: Quiet Birdmen, a social organization for men who are or have been licensed pilots (Harold E. Baughman, Baughman's Aviation Dictionary and Reference Guide [Glendale, CA.: Aero, 1940] 141); (see note 31.26).

61.7 transport ratings: The license or rating given an applicant permitting him to pilot airplanes or carry goods for hire. This rating, "the most demanding of all pilots' certificates, required 1200 hours of solo flying, including 500 hours of cross-country, and 75 solo hours of night flying" (Harrison 160).

61.9-10 chromium-Geddes sanctuary: Like a building that Norman Bel Geddes (1893-1958), an architect who was active and particularly well-known during the thirties, might have designed. He began as an innovator in theatre design with his radically simple sets, moved on to industrial design in the thirties, and eventually became interested in transportation and became identified with the concept of streamlining (see note 88.21); (Carol Willis, "Norman Bel Geddes," MacMillan Encyclopedia of Architecture, 2 vols., ed. Adolf K. Placzek, [New York: Free Press, 1982] 2: 182).

61.29 pressing clubs: The cloth-covered forms placed inside tailored clothes during the process of steam pressing them.

62.1-3 a Spanish jar filled with the sand pocked by
chewinggum and cigarettes and burnt matches: (See also notes
63.6-7 and 69.22.) The image of the vessel, sometimes perfect
and sometimes fouled, appears throughout Faulkner's work,
especially with reference to woman. Cf. Flags in the Dust
(completed in 1927). Horace has made himself "one almost
perfect vase of clear amber, larger, more richly and chastely
serene and which he kept always on his night table and called
by his sister's name in the intervals of apostrophising both
of them impartially in his moments of rhapsody over the
realization of the meaning of peace and the umblemished
attainment of it, as Thou still unravished bride of quietude"
([New York: Random House, 1973] 162). Cf. "Compson
Appendix," The Sound and the Fury. Quentin hated in Caddy
"what he considered the frail doomed vessel of its the
family's pride and the foul instrument of its disgrace." Cf.
As I Lay Dying (1930). Addie thinks of her lover, the
Reverend Whitfield: "I would think about his name until after
a while I could see the word as a shape, a vessel, and I
could watch him liquefy and flow into it like the cold
molasses flowing out of the darkness into the vessel, until
the jar stood full and motionless: a significant shape
profoundly without life like an empty doorframe, and then I
find that I had forgotten the name of the jar. The shape of
my body where I used to be a virgin is in the shape of a"
([New York: Vintage Books, 1964] 165). Cf. Light in August.
Joe Christmas, after an encounter with Bobbie, the waitress,

"seemed to see a diminishing row of suavely shaped urns in moonlight, blanched. And not one was perfect. Each one was cracked and from each crack there issued something liquid, deathcolored, and foul. He touched a tree, leaning his propped arms against it, seeing the ranked and moonlit urns. He vomited" (177-178). Also in Light in August, Hightower describes woman as "the receptacle" of the seed (442). Cf. Absalom, Absalom! where woman is described as "hollow" ([New York: Random House, 1936] 145). Horace's vase is, of course, an allusion to Keats' Grecian urn, but this passage from Flags in the Dust also resembles a comparison Faulkner made between his work and a vase. In an introduction he wrote for a 1933 edition of The Sound and the Fury he said, "Now I can make myself a vase like that which the old Roman kept at his bedside and wore the rim slowly away with kissing it" (Southern Review 8[1972]: 710). In another version of that introduction he writes, "There is a story somewhere about an old Roman who kept at his bedside a Tyrrhenian vase which he loved and the rim of which he wore slowly away with kissing it. I had made myself a vase, but I suppose I knew all the time that I could not live forever inside it, that perhaps to have it so that I too could lie in bed and look at it would be better . . ." (Mississippi Quarterly 26[1973]: 415). Meriwether points out (The Faulkner Newsletter & Yoknapatwpha Review 2[1982]: 2, 4) that the Tyrrhenian vase comes from H. Sienkiewicz's Quo Vadis: "Bronzebeard loves song, especially his own; and old Scaurus his Corinthian vase, which stands

near his bed at night, and which he kisses when he cannot
sleep. He has kissed the edge off already" ([Boston: Little
Brown, 1897] 6). Of course, the image of the woman as vessel
is Freudian. "The female genitalia are symbolically
represented by all such objects as share with them the
property of enclosing a space or are capable of acting as
receptacles: such as pits, hollows and caves, and also jars
and bottles" (Sigmund Freud, A General Introduction to
Psycho-Analysis: A Course of Twenty-Eight Lectures Delivered
at the University of Vienna [New York: Liveright, 1920; 1935]
139).

62.25-27 thinking how he had not expected to see her again
because tomorrow and tomorrow do not count: also in Pylon
"When I have had some coffee, it will be tomorrow . . . then
it is already tomorrow and so you dont have to wait for it"
(107); "And tomorrow it's just a hangover; you aint still
drunk tomorrow: tomorrow you can't feel this bad," (108);
chapter titles "Tomorrow" (113) and "And Tomorrow" (167);
"tomorrow and tomorrow and tomorrow; not only to hope, not
even to wait: just to endure" (284). The allusion echoes
throughout Faulkner's work. Cf. Soldiers' Pay: "Mr.
Saunders gave it up. To-morrow, he promised himself. Tomorrow I will do it" (175). "Then the singing died, fading
away along the mooned land inevitable with to-morrow and
sweat, with sex and death and damnation" ([New York: Boni &
Liveright, 1926] 319). Cf. The Sound and the Fury, where

Quentin tells Shreve, "I'm not doing anything. Not until tomorrow, now" (125). Cf. <u>Light in August</u>. After an encounter with Joanna Burden, Christmas thinks: "And going on: Tomorrow night, all the tomorrows, to be a part of the flat pattern, going on. He thought of that quiet astonishment: going on, myriad, familiar, since all that had ever been was the same as all that was to be, since tomorrow to-be and had-been would be the same. Then it was time" (226). Hightower thinks, "that the week to come, which will begin tomorrow, is the abyss" (348). Faulkner probably alludes to <u>Macbeth</u>, V.v: "She should have died hereafter;/ There would have been time for such a word./ To-morrow, and to-morrow, and to-morrow/ Creeps in this petty pace from day to day/ To the last syllable of recorded time,/ And all our yesterdays have lighted fools/ The way to dusty death. Out, out brief candle!/ Life's but a walking shadow, a poor player/ That struts his hour upon the stage/ And then is heard no more. It is a tale/ Told by an idiot, full of sound and fury,/ Signifying nothing" (1133).

63.6-7 Basque chamberpot: The Basques are a people who live in both Spain and France in areas bordering the Bay of Biscay and encompassing the western foothills of the Pyrenees. Physically they resemble Western Europeans, and they are devout Roman Catholics (<u>New Encyclopaedia Britannica</u>: <u>Micropaedia</u>, 1980 ed.). The reporter has substituted

"Basque" for "Spanish" and "chamberpot" for "jar" as he describes the vessel for his editor (see notes 62.1-3 and 69.22).

63.14-16 Bornean whatsitsname that has to spawn running to keep from being devoured by its own litter: The Greek deity Chronos (Time) is said to have devoured his own children, just as time, which, "as it brings an end to all things which have had a beginning, may be said to devour its own offspring" (Bulfinch 5).

63.17-18 blue serge suit: The standard business suit of the time; everyday work clothes for the affluent, but a luxury for a poor man. Serge is a fabric of "wool, cotton, silk, or rayon, twill weave . . . most popular as navy-blue worsted suiting" (Charlotte Calasibetta, Fairchild's Dictionary of Fashion [New York: Fairchild, 1975] 204).

63.23 one thousand . . . . nights: These ellipses stand for " cuntless." Faulkner originally substituted "womanless" for the "cuntless" that appeared in the galley proofs. But he has crossed through his first change and noted in the margin--"Period for each letter in 'cuntless'."

64.5 No news is good newspaper news: A perversion of the old saying, "No news is good news"; the reporter is suggesting that newspapers rarely contain any significant information.

64.14 new gray homburg hat: "The aristocrat of felt hats for men" (Doreen Yarwood, Costume of the Western World [New York: St. Martin's, 1980] 118), a luxury item even for an affluent man. This hat is "soft felt with narrow rolled brim and soft dented crown," worn from the 1870s on for formal daytime occasions (Calasibetta 272).

64.19-22 like an early Briton who has been assured that the Roman governor will not receive him unless he wear the borrowed centurion's helmet: Britons here are the Celts who lived in ancient Britain before the Roman invasion; centurion refers to an officer in the Roman army.

65.26 kikes: A derogatory term for Jews.

66.7 General Behindman: General Feinman (see note 14.22-23).

66.12 assscratcher: Slang meaning that all this bureaucrat bothers to do is scratch himself.

65.15 guttapercha: A rubbery material used for insulation and derived from the tropical guttapercha tree (see note 11.28).

67.7 ambulancechaser: He is the kind of reporter who will follow an ambulance to the scene of an accident or disaster in order to get a story. This slang term is usually used to describe unethical or overly-aggressive lawyers.

67.19 sciatica: Chronic pain in the hip or thigh, usually associated with aging.

68.4 skirt: Slang for woman.

68.18 berries: Slang for dollars

68.23 whole twenty bucks was velvet: Slang meaning the twenty dollars was pure profit.

69.22 greaser chamberpot: Greaser is a derogatory term probably meaning Italian or Spanish, like greaseball, which is used to refer to "Latin immigrant men who wore a lot of grease in their hair" (Anita Pearl, Dictionary of Popular Slang [New York: Jonathan David, 1980] 62). The reporter has now substituted "greaser" for "Basque" (see notes 62.1-3 and 63.6-7).

69.23-24 these kind of coats that look like they need a shave bad: In a letter to Miss Maud from England in October of 1925, Faulkner wrote, "I've got the best looking sport-jacket you ever saw. It is of hand-woven Harris tweed and has every possible color in it . . . . It does look like it needs a shave though" (Blotner, Faulkner 476).

70.6 Amboise Street: Brooks writes, "Amboise is probably meant to be another street in the Quarter, but I have no guess as to its real equivalent" (401). Amboise is a town in west central France, on the Loire River, noted for its late Gothic Castle where Leonardo Da Vinci is said to be buried (Seltzer 60).

71.7 Lanier Avenue: Lanier is probably Claiborne Avenue, "to judge from where it crosses Grandlieu (Canal) St." (Brooks 401).

71.14 galluses: Suspenders.

72.9 beat the bus: Slang for rode the bus for free.

72.22 long haul: Slang for a long ride.

73.7 Pullman extra fare: The fare for the sleeping car is more than for the passenger car.

74.4 cuddy: A small room or cupboard.

75.4 Shoot: Slang meaning tell me.

75.17-18 scarehead: A newspaper term for a large headline used for sensational news.

77.6 dawn's whitewings: Cf. Poem "VI," Vision in Spring, where "The dark ascends/ Lightly on pale wings of folding light" (36).

77.7 Momus' Nilebarge: John B. Vickery points out that a
similar use of these two terms occurs in Sir Philip Sidney's
An Apoloy for Poetry: "but if (fie on such a but) you be
borne so neere the dull making Cataphract of Nilus that you
cannot heare the Plannet-like Music of Poetrie, if you have
so earth-creeping a mind that it cannot lift it selfe up to
looke to the sky of Poetry, or rather, by a certain rusticall
disdaine, will become such a Mome as to be a Momus of Poetry"
("William Faulkner and Sir Philip Sidney?" Modern Language
Notes 70[1955]: 349-350).

77.7 Momus': This Mardi Gras parade, named after Momus--"the
faultfinder of Olympus; god of adverse criticism,
faultfinding, mockery and pleasantry" (Serafin 167)--is one
of the Big Four, also including Comus, Proteus, and Rex.
Begun in 1872, this parade is traditionally held on the
Thursday night before Mardi Gras (Goreau 354), as it is in
Pylon the day before the novel begins and the day of the
dedication of Feinman Airport. Early in its history, it was
known for some biting political satire (Goreau 352-353).

77.7 Nilebarge: Cf. Shakespeare's Antony and Cleopatra,
II.ii. Enobarbus describes Cleopatra's barge: "The barge she
sat in, like a burnished throne,/ Burned on the water: the
poop was beaten gold;/ Purple the sails, and so perfumed

that/ The winds were lovesick with them; the oars were silver" (1182). Faulkner refers here to the floats (see note 53.22-23), which are barge-like creations of papier-mâché and tinsel which quiver and glitter as they move very slowly through the streets of New Orleans. Cleopatra is also present in "A Game of Chess," T. S. Eliot's "The Waste Land" (Collected Poems 73).

77.7 clatterfalque: Catafalque, the raised structure upon which a coffin rests during a state funeral. Thomas McHaney points out that this is a favorite image of Faulkner's and cites several examples (William Faulkner: The Wild Palms: A Study [Jackson: UP of Mississippi, 1975] 32). Cf. The Wild Palms: "stinking catafalque of the dead corpse" (139); "catafalque of invincible dream" (149). Cf. Absalom, Absalom!: "Then Ellen died. . .the substanceless shell . . . no body to be buried: just the shape, the recollection, translated on some peaceful afternoon without bell or catafalque into that cedar grove" (126).

77.9 drill: Heavy cotton twill used for work clothes (Calasibetta 190).

77.13-16 like a scarecrow weathered gradually out of the earth which had supported it erect and intact and now poised for the first light vagrant air to blow it into utter dissolution: Cf. Psalms 35:5: "Let them . . . be as chaff

before the wind: and let the angel of the Lord chase them."
Cf. Psalms 1:4, where "The ungodly . . . are like the chaff
which the wind driveth away." Cf. "The Hollow Men," T. S.
Eliot: "Let me also wear/ Such deliberate disguises/ Rat's
skin, crowskin, crossed staves/ In a field/ Behaving as the
wind behaves" (<u>Collected Poems</u> 102).

77.20-22 apocryphal nighttime batcreatures whose nest or home
no man ever saw, which are seen only in midswoop: Vampires,
the un-dead who survive beyond the grave by feeding on human
blood obtained when they pierce their victims' jugulars with
their sharp pointed teeth. The ability of the vampire to
transform himself into a bat, though a popularly held notion,
is not traditional, rather the fabrication of Bram Stoker,
author of <u>Dracula</u> (1897) (Donald F. Glut, <u>The Dracula Book</u>,
[Metuchen, NJ: Scarecrow, 1975] 22). Vampires are usually
described or depicted as deathly pale, but with cheeks
flushed after they have fed on the blood of their victims.
Though Bram Stoker's Count Dracula is tall and aristocratic
and dressed entirely in black--as is Bela Lugosi's Dracula of
the 1931 Universal production, "Dracula"--Count Orlock of Max
Schrenk's 1922 film, "Nosferatu" (released in this country in
1929), is a "bald, human rodent, resuscitated from some foul
smelling grave, moving stiffly as if impaired by the
restrictions of rigor mortis. He wore no tuxuedo or cloak,
but a simple contemporary suit, the long coat buttoned up the
front" (Glut 103). Traditionally, vampires spend the daylight

hours in a death-like sleep in their coffins, Count Dracula in a coffin filled with soil from his native country, Transylvania. Dracula particularly likes to victimize beautiful young women, who swoon as if with sexual pleasure when he bites.

78.20 wingfabric: The wings of early biplanes, the Jenny for instance, were actually wooden frameworks covered in tightly-stretched, closely-woven linen or cotton (see note 21.2).

78.30 bowieknife: A large hunting knife adapted especially for knife-fighting. It has a guarded handle; its blade is 10 to 15 inches long, single-edged, the back of the blade straight for most of its length, then curving concavely and sometimes in a sharpened edge to its point. The knife is named for James Bowie (1790?-1836), a colonel in the Texas army who was killed at the Alamo.

80.1 irongrilled balconies: The iron balconies and fences of the French Quarter are often referred to as grillework (see note 15.21).

80.16-19 Lethe itself just behind them and they four shades this moment out of the living world and being hurried . . . toward complete oblivion: They have entered Hades (Serafin 90).

80.16 Lethe: The river of forgetfulness in Hades.

80.16 shades: "The disembodied spirits of Hades" (Serafin 173).

81.8 Toulouse: As Brooks has already pointed out, this is "the real name of a street in the French Quarter" (401). The street, named after the Compte de Toulouse, an illegitimate son of Louis XIV, was originally the site of fashionable homes and of banks and cotton brokers, "the Wall Street of old New Orleans" (Lyle Saxon, Fabulous New Orleans [New York: Century, 1928] 275). By the time of Saxon's book, the once-grand Court of Two Lions had become a rooming house with a second-hand furniture shop (275); in 1938 the City Guide described the site of the French Opera House as "boarded up and used by a wrecking company as a parking lot" (241).

81.9 Our house: They had stayed in a hotel which was actually a brothel.

83.3-4 sound, of revelry: This would be the crowds cheering the parade floats as they passed, their screaming for the trinkets tossed out by the maskers riding the floats (see note 53.22-23).

83.8-10 a tilefloored and walled cavern containing nothing, like an incomplete gymnasium showerroom, and lined with two

rows of discreet curtained booths: Cf. Mosquitoes: "Where was
once a dingy foodladen room, wooden floored and not too
clean, was now a tiled space cleared and waxed for dancing
and enclosed on one side by mirrors and on the other by a row
of booths containing each a table and two chairs and lighted
each by a discreet table lamp . . . and curtained each with
heavy maroon" (296).

83.11 faunfaced: Fauns are Roman satyrs, a "class of rural
deities, half goat, half man, or of human shape, with pointed
ears, horns, and a goat's tail" (Serafin 161). Cf. The
Marble Faun (1860), Nathaniel Hawthorne: "The character of
the face" of the Faun of Praxiteles "is most agreeable in
outline and feature, but rounded and somewhat voluptuously
developed, especially about the throat and chin; the nose is
almost straight, but very slightly curves inward, thereby
acquiring an indescribable charm of geniality and humor. The
mouth, with its full yet delicate lips, seems so nearly to
smile outright that it calls forth a responsive smile" ([New
York: New American Library, 1961] 15). The Marble Faun, a
collection of pastoral poems published in 1924, was
Faulkner's first book.

83.13-14 absinth: A liqueur, yellowish-green, highly
aromatic, dry and somewhat bitter in taste. The herb
"Wormwood . . . is the chief flavouring ingredient; the other
aromatic ingredients include licorice, usually perdominating

in the aroma," and other herbs (<u>Britannica</u>: <u>Micropaedia</u>).
Though it is now believed that the very high alcohol content
of absinthe makes it dangerous, earlier it was supposed that
wormwood caused "hallucinations, mental deterioration, and
sterility"; thus absinthe was outlawed in many countries,
first in Switzerland in 1908 and eventually in the United
States. While the 1938 <u>City Guide</u> included recipes for
dripped absinthe and the Sazerac Cocktail, made with
absinthe, Saxon writes in 1928 that drinks like the "absinthe
frappe and the absinthe-anisette" are "dear, forbidden
beverages . . . gone from us now" (261). Absinthe was also
"the traditional drink of the literary and artistic circle in
Paris in the 19th century" (John Doxat, <u>The Book of Drinking</u>,
[London: Triune, 1973] 35). William Spratling (see note
57.8), in his introduction to the 1966 facsimile edition of
<u>Sherwood Anderson & Other Famous Creoles</u>, writes that one
could always find at Lyle Saxon's house in New Orleans "a
dozen or so writers and painters or musicians and actresses
or caricaturists and a big pitcher of absinthe and good
conversation" (12).

83.16 Mardi Gras tourists: The <u>Louisiana Guide</u> (1941) reports
100,000 tourists yearly from all over the United States and
the world for Mardi Gras. New Orleans' restaurateurs, hotel
and bar owners were notorious then as now for openly raising
their prices when tourists came to town.

83.16 Pete: Pete appears in _Mosquitoes_, the son of an Italian family and in the restaurant business, though in the earlier novel Pete's older brother Joe runs the restaurant and wears the silk shirt (298). _Pylon_'s Pete has "a shock of black curls" and "a pair of eyes like two topazes" (83). Likewise the Pete of _Mosquitoes_ has "thickly curling hair" and "queer golden eyes" (300), a characteristic both share with Januarius Jones of _Soldiers' Pay_, whose eyes are "clear and yellow" (67).

83.18 mike: Used in direct address to mean man or fellow.

83.30 mamma: The old lady, Pete's mother, is present in _Mosquitoes_ also, though she avoids rather than participates in the family business. Cf. _Mosquitoes_, 296-300. Perhaps both were suggested to Faulkner by the mother of a bootlegger for whom he said he worked in the early 1920s: "she was an Italian, she was a nice little old lady, and she was an expert, she would turn it [raw alcohol] into Scotch with a little creosote, or bourbon" (_Faulkner in the University_ 21).

84.2-3 a gallon jug of something without color: Grain alcohol, used especially during Prohibition to fake various kinds of liquor (see note 83.30).

84.6 paregoric: "Camphorated tincture of opium, taken internally for the relief of diarrhea and intestinal pain"

(The American Heritage Dictionary of the English Language, 1978 ed.). Paregoric mixed into grain alcohol was a common substitute for the illegal absinthe. Saxon remarks that "some sort of substitutes are dispensed illegally occasionally," and remembers the first time he tasted absinthe, the flavor of which made him "wrinkle" his "nose and cry out, 'It's paregoric!'" (Fabulous New Orleans 261, 52).

84.12 madonna: "Formerly, an Italian title for a married woman, equivalent to Madam. It has been replaced in current usage by signora" (American Heritage Dictionary).

84.30 wild bright face: Cf. Flags in the Dust, where Narcissa gazes at young Bayard's twin, John Sartoris, whose "face was merry and wild" (63). Both brothers, for Narcissa, have an air of "smoldering abrupt violence," but "in John it was a warmer thing, spontaneous and merry and wild" (64).

85.28 shetland: Soft suiting fabric made of fine soft wool in gray, brown, black, or white from Shetland sheep of Scotland (Calasibetta 446).

86.5 Yale or perhaps a Cornell senior: Both Yale and Cornell are Ivy League schools, academically exclusive and expensive.

86.12 roadster: An open car with two seats in front and a rumble seat or trunk in the back.

86.12 hostler: Usually refers to one who cares for horses.

87.2 rumble: "Rumble-seat, an automobile seat, with a fold-down top which forms the backrest, placed where the trunk is on most present-day cars" (Brown 165).

87.11-16 A machine expensive, complex, delicate and intrinsically useless, created for some obscure psychic need of the species if not the race, from the virgin resources of a continent, to be the individual muscles bones and flesh of a new and legless kind: This passage prefigures Faulkner's review of November, 1935, in American Mercury, of Test Pilot by Jimmy Collins. Faulkner writes of a new "species or race . . . trained to conduct the vehicles in which the rest of us will hurtle from place to place . . . . These would be a species and in time a race and in time they would produce a folklore" (Essays, Speeches and Public Letters by William Faulkner, ed. James B. Meriwether [New York: Random House, 1966] 189).

87.17-18 cryptic shields symbolic of laughter and mirth: Earlier he refers to the "cryptic shieldcaught (i n r i) loops of bunting" (P 86 and see also note 60.11). Here he seems to be referring to the shield-like, smiling mask that the Greeks wore when performing comedy and that has come to represent the comic theater.

88.21 streamlining: A catch-word of the thirties, streamlining, which means minimizing air resistance, was important in the design of automobiles, locomotives, and airplanes but also came to be applied to industrial design and architecture. The streamlined style was considered very modern (see note 61.9-10).

90.11-26 That room . . . which the reporter called bohemian . . . cut into two uneven halves . . . by an old theatre curtain . . . cluttered with slovenly mended and useless tables draped with imitation batik bearing precarious lamps made of liquorbottles, and other objects of oxidised metal made for what original purpose no man knew, and hung with more batik and machine-made Indian blankets and indecipherable basrelief plaques vaguely religio-Italian primitive: Possibly this spoofs not only the bohemian but also the gothic interior, as in Stoker's Dracula (see note 77.20-22): "The table service is of gold, and so beautifully wrought that it must be of immense value. The curtains and upholstery of the chairs and sofas and the hangings of my bed are of the costliest and most beautiful fabrics" ([New York: Grosset & Dunlap, 1897] 18).

90.18 Vieux Carré: (See note 57.8.)

90.21 batik: Fabric dyed by the batik method in which a design is drawn on silk or cotton, then all areas which are to remain white are covered with wax, the fabric is dyed, wax removed, resulting in a pattern with a cracked effect, usually dark blue, rust, black, or yellow (Calasibetta 26).

90.22-23 objects of oxidised metal: Statuettes in bronze influenced by "dynamic motifs (figures with flowing hair or clothes, gazelles, greyhounds)" and stylized animal and human figures were mass-produced in the twenties. Gorham, for example, established a bronze foundry around 1925 for manufacturing small human and animal figures (The Collector's Encyclopedia: Victorian/Art Deco [London: Collins, 1974] 24, 124). Like the "imitation batik" and "machine-made Indian blankets" (90), these are manufactured works of "art."

90.25-26 basrelief plaques: "A form of sculpture in which the figures project but slightly from the general background." The frieze of the Parthenon is a good example (Russell Sturgis, A Dictionary of Architecture and Building [New York: MacMillan, 1901] 1: 235).

91.9-10 evolved by forced draft in a laboratory and both beyond and incapable of any need for artificial sustenance: I am unsure what Faulkner means by forced draft; however, Frankenstein's monster (Frankenstein; or, The Modern Prometheus, 1818) was created in a laboratory, though Mary

Shelley is extremely vague about how the monster's creator brought him to life. The reporter and the monster have two other things in common: both are walking, breathing corpses, one literally, one figuratively; and neither has a past.

91.4-5 theatrical morgue: A theater's collection of old costumes, props, and sets.

91.11 tumbleweed: Any of various plants, the best-known of which is the ball-shaped Russian thistle, which at the time the seeds mature break off at the groundline and then are blown about the desert or prairie (Encyclopedia Americana, 1984 ed.).

92.13 mustard gas: A chemical-warfare weapon that was first used in WWI, dispersed as a gas by a bursting shell, causing severe blistering and very irritating to the eyes (Encyclopedia Americana).

92.25-93.3 He saw all this beneath a plump rich billowing of pink plumes so that he thought of himself looking at a canvas out of the vernal equinox of pigment when they could not always write to sign their names to them--a canvas conceived in and executed out of that fine innocence of sleep and open bowels capable of crowning the rich foul unchaste earth with rosy cloud where lurk and sport oblivious and incongruous cherubim: Possibly a reference to early 18th-century French art, the rococo style; for example, the paintings of Watteau and Fragonard.

95.26 dance marathons at six A.M.: Dance marathons were a craze that started in the twenties and continued into the thirties. The object of the contest was to see which dancers could stay on their feet the longest, and the contests would continue through the night into the morning. These marathons often became sad affairs during the thirties when couples danced for the prize money they desperately needed. Obviously, this is the reporter's elaborate way of saying that his mother is no longer young.

97.1 the pirate Lafitte: Jean Lafitte, who came to New Orleans in 1804, operated a blacksmith shop with his brother Pierre, which was a front for disposing of smuggled goods by 1809, and had organized a band of smugglers and pirates at Barataria Bay off the Louisiana coast by 1811. Lafitte and his pirates became heroes when they fought bravely for the American cause in the Battle of New Orleans (Louisiana: A Guide 418-419). According to Grace King, Jean Lafitte was handsome, charming, spoke several languages fluently, and "possessed in a high degree that shining substitute for education, an invaluable gift to the unscrupulous money maker, the art of making phrases" (New Orleans: The Place and the People [New York: MacMillan, 1911] 190).

97.23-24 an hour's dual: Dual time is flight-time with an instructor. The reporter has had an hour of flight instruction. According to Harrison, during this first hour the instructor demonstrates "climbs, turns, level flight, and descents, while the student merely rests his hands and feet lightly on the controls, 'following through' the various manoeuvres" (161).

98.1-5 because Laverne and Roger have gone to bed in the bed with the kid and so maybe him and Jack are trying to get boiled enough to sleep on the floor: Cf. "The Dumb Man," Triumph of the Egg. In Anderson's poem three men are in a room in a house while upstairs there is a woman "who craved love." Eventually two of the men lie down on the floor to sleep as a fourth man, who "may have been Death," enters the house and goes up to the woman. Of the men downstairs, one, like Jack, is handsome with a narrow moustache (see note 19.16); another is "dog-like," an image associated with both Jiggs (P 245) and the reporter (P 91); ([New York: Huebsch, 1921] 1-4).

98.4 boiled: Drunk, along with stewed and fried (Wentworth 50).

98.8 dive: "A disreputable, cheap, low-class establishment or public place, esp. a bar, dance-hall, nightclub" (Wentworth 151).

98.11-12 with a bathtub and enough grain alcohol and a bottle or paregoric or maybe it's laudanum: This is precisely how the reporter's absinthe was made (see notes 84.2-3 and 84.6), though paregoric rather than laudanum was probably used to flavor the alcohol (see notes 83.13-14, 83.30, and 84.2-3).

100.28 bootjack: A wooden or metal v-shaped device used in pulling off boots. This instrument becomes a phallic symbol in the travestied love scene that follows (P 100-104).

102.4 listening to himself laughing . . . "I'm trying to quit. But I can't": Cf. The Sound and the Fury. Quentin "began to laugh again. I could feel it in my throat . . . . But still I couldnt stop it and then I knew that if I tried too hard to stop it I'd be crying" (182-183). Cf. Sanctuary Temple "began to laugh . . . . Then she quit laughing by holding her breath" (43). Cf. As I Lay Dying. Darl's laughter is a sign of his madness, at least as his family sees it (223, 243-244).

102.22 homemade putties: In WWI, leggings made of long strips of khaki wool wrapped around the leg from ankle to knee, later made of shaped pieces of fabric or leather and closed with buckles, like gaiters (Calasibetta 416).

107.20 Market: The French Market. One of the oldest institutions in New Orleans, its five buildings were divided

into numerous stalls where meat, fish, and produce were
sold. It extends along Decatur and N. Peter Streets from
Barracks to St. Ann Street. There were and are coffee shops
at either end of the Market (see also note 15.24-26). The
City Guide describes it thus: "The busy rush of trucks and
wagons, the ceaseless babble of foreign tongues, the strange
mixture of humanity ebbing and flowing, and the confusion of
odors give a setting and atmosphere truly characteristic of
the Old French city" (255). When Faulkner lived in New
Orleans in 1925, he "rose early each morning and often went
to a coffee stand in the French Market down near the river.
It was fashionable to end a night's gaiety with the strong
black coffee, and mornings after gala Mardi Gras balls men
and women in evening dress would sit before the high mirrors
drinking the steaming, chicory-flavored brew" (Blotner,
Faulkner 525).

107.24 Latin faces: The Spanish and French are original
settlers of New Orleans, and they and their descendants, the
Creoles, once exclusively occupied the French Quarter.
According to the City Guide, "Some of the Creole families
cling to their old quarter, but the Vieux Carré, especially
around the French Market, is now an Italian district" (43).

109.6 "Qu'est-ce qu'il voulait?": This translates from the
French as "What does he want?" (see note 107.24).

109.8 "D'journal d'matin": French for "The morning paper."

109.9 "Donne-t-il": French for "Give it to him."

113.17 try to ride him: To tease or nag him (Wentworth 426).

114.24 check them valves: Measure the valve stems (see notes 19.8) for proper length and diameter (see also notes 116.21-22 and 124.2-3). Valves control the flow of intake and exhaust gases to and from the cylinders.

115.10 slop jar: "A large bucket-shaped chamber pot used, in the absence of plumbing, for both urine and waste water from the washbasin. Sometimes there was a separate chamber pot" (Brown 180).

116.21-22 valves miked: Measure with a micrometer. Valves which have stretched or expanded must be replaced (see notes 114.24 and 124.2-3). A micrometer is a device used for measuring such minute dimensions.

117.21 starting out on a bat today: A bat is a drinking spree (Wentworth 22).

117.26 in a jam: Slang for in trouble.

117.27-28 Main Street: Jiggs refers here to Grandlieu (see

note 11.19) where they would need to go to catch a bus out to the airport.

118.8-10 a bed neatly madeup, so neatly restored that it shouted the fact that it had been recently occupied by a woman who did not live there: Cf. Sanctuary: "Lying together there," Ruby and her baby "lent to the room a quality of transience more unmistakable than the make-shift light, the snug paradox of the made bed in a room otherwise redolent of long unoccupation. It was as though femininity were a current running through a wire" (95).

118.30 the moral and spiritual waif shrieking his feeble I-am-I: Cf: Light in August: Byron "approached the bed. The still invisible occupant snored profoundly. There was a quality of profound and complete surrender in it. Not of exhaustion, but surrender, as though he had given over and relinquished completely that grip upon the blending of pride and hope and vanity and fear, that strength to cling either to defeat or victory, which is the I-am, the relinquishment of which is usually death" (372).

119.10 safetywire: A flexible brass or copper wire used to prevent nuts, bolts, or turnbuckle barrels from turning.

119.24-25 there is some crap I will not eat: Slang for there are some things to which he will not stoop. Cf. "i sing of

Olaf glad and big" (1930), e. e. cummings: "Olaf (upon what were once knees)/ does almost ceaselessly repeat/ 'there is some shit I will not eat'" (Complete Poems: 1913-1962, [New York: Harcourt Brace Jovanovich, 1972] 339).

123.1 on your ass: Clearly Jack feels that they are taking advantage of the reporter's desire for Laverne by accepting his offer of a place to stay.

124.2-3 a valvestem has stretched . . . That must be why she ran hot yesterday: According to Harrison, the fact that Shumann's engine overheated suggests that the valves are stuck, that they have expanded. The bad valves need to be pulled, ground to correct dimensions, and replaced. Since this job is never done, the engine overheats again in the next race (161); (see notes 114.24, 116.21-22, and 163.9-10).

124.12-13 hung up: Delayed, detained, or "stymied by a problem" (Wentworth 277).

126.23-24 deadheaded: Deadhead can mean a nonpaying spectator (Wentworth 142). Jack had no money; Jiggs must mean that he found a free ride out to the airport. In charter flying a deadhead "is that portion of a trip made without paying passenger or cargo" (Harrison 161).

126.27 If things break right today: If things go well today.

This slang use of break probably comes from billiards where the balls may break advantageously.

128.3 sticklike arm . . . a bundle of dried twigs too: Cf. As I Lay Dying: "Beneath the quilt" Addie "is no more than a bundle of rotten sticks" (43). Cf. "The Unvanquished" and The Unvanquished: Grandmother Millard "had looked little alive, but now she looked like she had collapsed, like she had been made out of a lot of little thin dry light sticks notched together and braced with cord, and now the cord had broken and all the little sticks had collapsed in a quiet heap on the floor" (Saturday Evening Post 14 Nov. 1936; The Unvanquished 175).

128.16-18 the waitress' arm propped beside him, wrist-nestled by four woolworth bracelets: Cf. "The Love Song of J. Alfred Prufrock," T. S. Eliot: "And I have known the arms already, known them--/ Arms that are braceleted and white and bare" (Collected Poems 14).

128.17-18 woolworth bracelets: Dime-store bracelets. Woolworth's was a chain of five-and-ten-cent stores, still in business today, where a variety of inexpensive items were sold.

129.3 dungarees: Work pants named for the coarse blue fabric from which they are made (Calasibetta 383).

129.6 sandwich board: Like the signs worn by sandwich men who paraded through the streets sandwiched between boards containing advertisements.

130.14 engine mount: A large tab upon which the engine is mounted.

131.16-17 clean out the supercharger: Particles of dust which build up on the intake side of a supercharger (see note 22.5) must be removed (Harrison 161) so air flow to the engine will not be restricted, decreasing its power.

133.8-9 motion limber and boneless and softly rapacious as that of an octopus: In Flags in the Dust Belle's hand is described as "prehensile" (180).

136.24 beaverboard: Particleboard. An inexpensive building material used for walls and partitions.

138.12 Leonora: William Spratling had a "slatternly but glorious cook named Leonore" (Sherwood Anderson & Other Famous Creoles 12) working for him when Faulkner moved into his French Quarter apartment with him.

139.27 wearily initialled national fund: Roosevelt initiated many emergency relief and economic recovery programs during the Depression. Each was known by its initials, like the famous W.P.A., N.R.A., and C.C.C.

140.29-30 of that material which oldtime bookkeepers used to protect their sleeves with: Green felt.

141.10 Mash one!: The reporter is ordering a hot roast beef sandwich with mashed potatoes on top or on the side, gravy poured over all, rather than a plate lunch.

143.26 Sister: A slang term of direct address for a woman.

146.2 Columbus: (1451-1506) Italian-born explorer who, sailing from Spain, discovered America in 1492. Jiggs uses the name as a kind of slur since the man he is dealing with is obviously Italian.

149.22 ribbon badges: Evidence of military flight service.

151.5-7 Blinded . . . Couldn't read his altimeter at all . . . Flew it right into the ground: An altimeter is an instrument that measures the elevation of an aircraft (Baughman 25). The tendency in the absence of a height indicator is to fly down, eventually into the ground.

151.15 radial engine: Cylinders in a circle rather than in a line (see note 155.2).

154.30-155.2 a flight of army pursuit singleseaters circling the field in formation to land: Military pursuit planes are small, highly maneuverable, and very fast. They are designed "for quick climb and attack on enemy planes or protection of their own bombers" (Baughman 140). Demonstrations of tactical maneuvers and aerobatics by Army, Navy, or Marine Corps flyers were standard fare at airshows. The Times-Picayune reported that "a dozen new low-wing Boeing pursuit planes" would make up the tactical flight team which would be "a dandy feature" at the New Orleans air races. These planes were "far more powerful and speedier than any previous 'fighter'" (16 Feb. 1934: 3).

155.2 bluntnosed: Indicates that the plane is powered by a radial engine, a more powerful engine pound-for-pound than the in-line engine and easier to cool (see note 151.15).

155.2-3 fiercely-raked: Noses up, tails down. This is not an aviator's term.

155.3 oversouped: Too much engine for the airframe, dangerous, for one reason, because the aircraft could be overstressed, thus pulled apart.

155.13-14: she had put the supercharger back on with the engine head still off and the valves still out: Shumann and Jack will have to take the supercharger (see note 22.5) off and start all over, putting the valves in first (see notes 114.24, 116.21-22, and 124.2-3). This is a serious error on Laverne's part.

156.3 on the line: On the starting line.

157.14 beat it: Slang for go away.

163.9-10 Shumann's in trouble; he's out of the race . . . He's cut his switch: As Millgate has noted (The Achievement 140), at the air races Harold Neuman of Kansas City crash landed his plane when his motor stopped after he rounded a pylon (Times-Picayune 17 Feb. 1934: 1). Like Shumann, whose plane flipped over onto its back (P 164), Neuman "rolled" over in his plane; and, also like Shumann, he walked away from the accident uninjured with "his baby in his arms and his wife with her arm about him" (Times-Picayune 17 Feb. 1934: 1). (See also note 124.2-3.)

163.10 cut his switch: Shut off his engine to minimize any chance of fire in case he crashes (see note 163.19).

163.19 Hold her head up: Roger has cut his switch (see preceding note) and is making a deadstick landing. Without the thrust and the airflow created by the engine, the flight controls become much less effective. Gravity is pulling the plane down, particularly the heaviest part of the plane, the nose. Thus it is difficult to hold the nose up--necessary for a safe landing--with the engine dead.

164.7 undercarriage: British for landing gear, the under-structure which supports the weight of the airplane when on the ground and includes mechanisms for reducing the shock of landing, like the landing wheels (Baughman 106).

164.17-19 jumper limped over to him, dragging savagely the leg: Jack's injured leg is a characteristic he shares with quite a few of Faulkner's characters--Elmer, Byron Snopes, Quentin Compson, Cash Bundren, Sutpen's French architect, the ex-Marine in The Mansion, Ab Snopes, and the barber in "Dry September."

164.21-23 drifted by an unforseen windgust over the stands then slammed into one of the jerrybuilt refreshment booths: Jack's mishap parallels that of Eris Daniels during the actual New Orleans airshow. She "misjudged the strength of the west wind and fell into the lake. Miss Daniels missed the sea wall by two feet, and her parachute draped itself over the wall" (Times-Picayune, 17 Feb. 1934: 1).

164.22 jerrybuilt: Slang for makeshift, sloppily built.

164.30 If you want any satisfaction: This is the language of the duel, though, of course, Jack is not actually suggesting one.

165.9 Ninety-two: According to the local papers, Jimmy Wedell (see note 60.4) hoped to raise "his own world's speed record for land planes . . . with his famous '44'" (Times-Picayune 14 Feb. 1934: 1, 16) at the New Orleans races. He did break his own record in a modified "44" given the number "45" (Don Vorderman, The Great Air Races [Garden City, NY: Doubleday, 1969] 216). A Wedell-Williams plane did carry the number "92," but it was owned and raced by Johnny Worthen, though not in the New Orleans races as far as I can determine.

165.12 a bum: Anything considered useless or unsatisfactory (Wentworth 74).

167.10 valves went bad: (See notes 116.21-22, 124.2-3.)

167.14-15 the whole engine went: Because of the bad valves (see preceding note), the engine overheated and the pistons seized up.

167.15 rudderpost: The axle upon which the rudder pivots. The rudder is a control surface fitted to the trailing edge of the tailfin to provide directional control (Beckford 87).

167.15 longerons: Structural members that run from front to rear of an aircraft's fuselage.

168.24 Atkinson: Jimmy Wedell's (see notes 12.28, 60.4) business partner was Harry Williams.

169.19 a peanut: Peanuts is a slang term for a very small amount of money.

170.7-8 license revoked: In 1934 licensing was still a fairly new phenomenon in American aviation, coming in 1926 with the passage of the Air Commerce Act creating the Aeronautics Branch of the Department of Commerce. Thus pilots had to be licensed, planes inspected for airworthiness (C. R. Roseberry, The Challenging Skies [New York: Arno, 1980] 76). "Aircraft flown for racing purposes were issued special federal permits which were valid for one year" (Harrison 163).

170.8 the Department: (See preceding note.)

170.25 as parchment is made: The skins of sheep, goats, and calves are cleaned, stretched, and scraped to make parchment.

172.8 doped out: Figured out (Wentworth 156).

172.17 rebuild it; it wouldn't go fast enough: Nearly every new development in aeronautics between 1909 and 1931 was tied to air racing (Vorderman 9). Those racing insisted upon faster and faster planes, which meant experimenting with bigger, more powerful engines and aircraft design. Roscoe Turner, a Mississippian who dominated air racing for years in Wedell-Williams aircraft, wanted his final racing craft to possess "Power. Great reverberating heaps of it, attached to an airframe crafted from the finest materials and built just large enough to keep everything under control" (Vorderman 246). Cf. Flags in the Dust: Bayard Sartoris is told to "let that crate alone. These birds show up here every week with something that will revolutionize flying, some new kind of mantrap that flies fine--on paper" (356). The plane does crash, and Bayard is killed.

172.19 pull the engine: Take the engine out of the plane.

173.2-3 getting the license back on it: A new design had to be test-flown before it could be licensed (see note 170.7-8).

173.17 stressed it: Gave it a stress analysis test. "The determination of all the external applied loads and external reactions along with their respective magnitudes, directions and points of applications and the computation of the resultant internal stresses which occur in the elements of the structure. In addition, the allowable stresses of the elements of structure must be determined and the margins of safety computed" (Baughman 167). In other words, the inspector computed mathematically whether or not the plane could withstand the stress of flying. According to Harrison, the inspector "tested the wings with weights" (163). A pilot may also stress a plane by flying it straight down and then pulling it out of the nose-dive.

173.28 stalled: At a certain speed and a very steep angle of climb, an aircraft will stall, causing loss of lift. The plane will sink rapidly before its nose drops and it goes into a spin. This maneuver is important in stunt flying as many rolls, loops, as well as spins begin in a stall. The ability of the pilot and plane to recover from a stall is necessary for licensing (Baughman 268). "No specific demonstration of stall characterics was required," according to Harrison (163).

174.1 getting the stick back: Pulling back the stick--the mechanism for steering the plane--should have pulled the nose up, but the controls had crossed and were behaving opposite to normal (see notes 174.5-7-174.21).

174.5-7 just jammed the stick forward like he was trying to dive it into the ground and sure enough the nose came up: Ord realized that the controls were behaving opposite to normal, so, rather than pulling the stick back, he shoved the stick forward to pull the nose up (see note 174.1).

174.8 slipstream: "A stream of air thrown rearwards by the screwing action of aircraft propellers" (L. L. Beckford, An A.B.C. of Aeronautics [London: Cassell, 1957] 92).

174.8 tailgroup: "The stabilizing and control surfaces at the rear end of an aircraft, including stabilizer, fin, rudder, and elevator" (Baughman 170).

174.9 Burble: The absence of normal air flow over the airplane's control surfaces--like the aileron on the wing or the rudder on the tail--negating or possibly even reversing the effect of the controls (see notes 174.1, 174.5-7).

174.11 being close to the ground: Harrison defines "ground effect" as the "cusion of air" beneath an airplane when it is within about "a wingspan of the earth" created by air washed downward by its wings (which also creates lift) (163). Ord has speculated that this phenomenon caused his plane to stall prematurely (164); (see note 174.21).

174.13 firewall: A fire-resistant wall which separates the engine from the rest of the plane and which would confine a fire to the engine compartment (Baughman 79).

174.15 gun: The throttle, which controls the speed of the airplane.

174.16 groundlooping: A ground loop is a horizontal spin, really a violent turn, on the ground during the landing or take-off runs (Baughman 91). The pilot is using this maneuver deliberately to slow down and stop.

174.21 weight distribution: Shumann suggests that the airplane is too nose-heavy; thus it is not possible "to keep the tail down in ground effect" (see note 174.11); (Harrison 164).

174.26 oleander: (<u>Nerium oleander</u>) An ancient shrub, characterized by "huge clusters of single or double flowers of a vanilla fragrance" which range from white through pink to red (Greene and Blomquist 171). "Since early French days, New Orleans has been noted for its oleanders. Their milky juice is poisonous . . . . A coarse, evergreen shrub with long narrow leaves, it reaches a height of 20'" (Greene and Blomquist 171); (see note 16.9).

174.27 palmettos: The common name for most kinds of palm trees. Faulkner probably refers to the cabbage palmetto (Sabal palmetto); (Brown 43).

175.25 ribbing me up: Slang for setting someone up, tricking or duping him.

176.5-18 Because it's thinking about the day after tomorrow . . . and even my towels: McHaney notes the similarity between this statement and Charlotte's argument for staying with Harry (94). Cf. The Wild Palms: "This is what it's for . . . what we were paying for: so we could be together, sleep together every night: not just to eat and evacuate and sleep warm again" (118-119).

178.12 set up: Newspaper jargon for set in type.

178.22 clean it: Clean it up (see note 179.24).

179.2 in the can: Slang for in jail.

179.7-11 Why dont you let these people alone? . . . I cant: Cf. Poor White, Sherwood Anderson, where Hugh felt "Again a hungry desire to enter into the lives of the people about him" (67). Anderson writes often of such a need. Winesburg, Ohio (1919), for instance, is story after story of one human being trying to make meaningful contact with another or others and usually being misunderstood or failing altogether.

179.19 clawlike hand: Cf. "The Love Song of J. Alfred Prufrock," T. S. Eliot: "I should have been a pair of ragged claws" (<u>Collected Poems</u> 14).

179.24 clean up the story: Newspaper jargon meaning edit it.

179.25 in galley: Newspaper jargon meaning already set in type.

180.17 Bayou Street: The map which accompanies the <u>City Guide</u> (1938) shows a Bayou Road which becomes Governor Nicholls Street in the Quarter and Gentilly Road at Grand Route St. John.

181.12 steak . . . on your eye: A home remedy for a black eye.

181.26 vag: To run in as a vagabond or vagrant (Partridge 755).

181.27 springing him: Slang for getting him out of jail by paying the fine.

183.26 oneway arrows: The streets in the French Quarter are so narrow that nearly all had been designated one-way.

184.19 wop stores: Wop is a derogatory term for a person of Italian descent. Around the French Market there were settlements of Italians (<u>City Guide</u> 44); Central Grocery, an old and well-known Italian grocery, was already operating across the street from the French Market at that time.

185.25 Noyades: Though Lyle Saxon writes that there was a Nayades as well as a Dryades Street, two of many named from pagan mythology (<u>Fabulous New Orleans</u> 285), I can find only Dryades in any city directory. "Noyades" actually means the "drownings" rather than "drowned." Brooks writes, "There is no street in New Orleans called Noyades. I suspect Faulkner evolved the name in some such fashion as this: There is a Dryades St., named for the Greek tree nymphs. This probably suggested to Faulkner a hypothetical Naiades St., the street of the sea nymphs. But he may have decided to go Naiades one better by turning it into Noyades St.--that is, the street of the drowned. Faulkner probably remembered a poem by Swinburne entitled 'Les Noyades.' This is the only way I can account for Hagood's translating the street name spelled out in the 'chipped mosaic' letters set in the curb as "The Drowned" (88).

185.18 chiaroscuro: "In drawing, painting, and the graphic arts, the rendering of forms through a balanced contrast between pronounced light and dark. The technique, which was introduced in the Renaissance, is effective in creating an illusion of depth and space around the principal figures in a composition. Leonardo and Rembrant were painters who excelled in its use" (Ralph Mayer, A Dictionary of Art Terms and Techniques [New York: Crowell, 1967] 72).

185.13-14 brown Rembrant gloom: Rembrant (1606-1669), Dutch painter, etcher, and draftsman, is famous for his fascination with light and shadow, particularly in his late works with their warm, deep crimson and golden yellow and predominantly dark brown backgrounds (Sir John Rothenstein, ed., New International Illustrated Enclopedia of Art [New York: Greystone, 1970] 3541). However, the recent cleaning of many Rembrants, like the famous and very dark "Night Watch," reveals that the gloom was not always Rembrant's intention, rather the result of "the layers of varnish that have been put on his paintings, obscuring their original values" (Rothenstein 3534).

188.24-25 It will qualify under five hundred and seventy-five cubic inches: The plane will technically qualify for this race but is much faster than the other planes entered.

188.25-26 loaf back on the throttle: The throttle controls the aircraft's speed; Shumann will use only half of the plane's potential for speed.

188.26-27 without having to make a vertical turn: A vertical turn is one in which the degree of bank is 70 to 90 degrees. Shumann thinks that he can still place in the race without banking in close to the pylons when he turns, by making a flat, wide turn, in other words.

188.28 the Trophy: The overall championship; the big-money race (see note 31.6-7).

189.11 controls cross: (See notes 174.1-174.15).

189.13 sandbags: Shumann will rig up weights which he can move about with some sort of pulley; moving them rearward will compensate for the plane's nose-heaviness and, possibly, make the plane "controllable" at low speed (Harrison 164); (see note 174.21).

189.16-17 move the pylons up to around four thousand feet: Flying at low altitudes is dangerous in any case, but especially with a plane that is oversouped (see notes 155.3, 188.24-25, and 188.25-26) and as difficult to control as this one apparently is. Flying at greater altitudes would increase Shumann's chances of leaving the plane or of landing safely if the plane were to go out of control and decrease the chances of his endangering other flyers and spectators.

191.23 the nightgown, the only silk one she had: Ruby, under her "cheap coat," wears a "lace-trimmed crepe nightgown" (Sanctuary 187).

192.17 celluloid comb and brush: Cheap, in other words. Celluloid was an early form of plastic (invented in 1869) primarily used as a substitute for ivory or tortoise shell (<u>Encyclopaedia Britannica</u>); (see note 11.28).

193.21 seawall: A wall built to prevent erosion of a shore. The sea wall mentioned here is part of the seven-mile wall along the New Orleans lake front, a project inaugurated by Huey Long. This sea wall "reclaimed many acres of swamp and enlarged the city's area . . . . The sea wall also served as a dike to protect the city from the backing up of the lake during floods and storms" (Roberts 338).

193.20 dead stick: (See notes 163.10 and 163.19).

193.21 mushing: Slang for coming in without power, "especially perilous" for Shumann because "the slightest downdraft would have sent him plunging into the sea wall" (Harrison 164).

194.17-20 climbing out onto the wing with the parachute harness buckled on and then dropping off and letting her own weight pull the parachute from the case attached to the wing: The earliest parachutes were of this automatic type, different from the ripcord type which Jack used and which allowed him to thrill the crowd with his free-fall (see note 27.19).

194.28 inner bay strut: A bay is a section of braced wing (Harrison 165). Laverne clings to a strut or brace (see note 45.3-4).

195.15-29 In the same instant of realising . . . the victorious: Cf. Poem "XIII," Helen: A Courtship (1926): "Two hawks there were, but proud and swift with flight/ One voided skies with passionate singleness,/ And he alone, in stricken ecstasy/ Locks beak to beak his shadowed keen distress/ In wild and cooling arc of death, and he/ is dead, yet darkly troubled down the night." (Helen: A Courtship and Mississippi Poems, New Orleans and Oxford, M: [Tulane U and Yoknapatawpha P, 1981] 124). Cf. Poem "XXV," A Green Bough: "O I have seen/ The ultimate howk unprop the ultimate skies,/ And with the curving image of his fall/ Locked beak to beak." ([New York: Harrison Smith and Robert Haas, 1933] 47; rpt. with The Marble Faun [New York: Random House, 1965]). Cf. Soldiers' Pay, where Januarius Jones says to Cecily, "Do you know how falcons make love? They embrace at an enormous height and fall locked, beak to beak, plunging: an unbearable ecstasy. While we have got to assume all sorts of ludicrous postures, knowing our own sweat. The falcon breaks his clasp and swoops away swift and proud and lonely, while a man must rise and take his hat and walk out" (227).

196.2-3 he remembered to roll the aeroplane toward the wing to which the parachute case was attached: "Had she fallen off the wrong side, the parachute would have been dragged over the fuselage and almost certainly have become entangled in the tail," causing the plane to crash (Harrison 165); (see note 299.5).

196.4 belt catching him: The belt catches him as he rolls the plane over to dump Laverne out of the cockpit (Harrison 165).

200.16-18 I'll pay you! . . . I'll pay her! I'll pay either of you . . . Let me . . . . her once and you can cut me if you want: Cf. The Hamlet, where Labove thinks of Eula: "And he did not want her as a wife, he just wanted her one time as a man with a gangrened hand or foot thirsts after the axe-stroke which will leave him comparatively whole again" ([New York: Random House, 1940] 134).

200.17 cut me: Probably a euphemism for castrate.

200.17 Let me . . . . her once: The ellipses here represent "fuck". Faulkner has crossed through "have" in the galley proofs and noted in the margin--"A period for each letter in 'fuck'."

201.5-6 blind landing: Generally a landing without external visibility; information for landing is obtained from instruments in the plane only. Since Shumann had to check his altitude against a "dimlyseen windmill" (P 201), it sounds as if he landed without visibility or instruments.

202.5 the butterflyspawn: While talking about Pylon at the University of Virginia in 1957, Faulkner described the flyers: "They were as ephemeral as the butterfly that's born this morning with no stomach and will be gone tomorrow" (Faulkner in the University 36).

202.6-7 Saint Jules Avenue: St. Charles Avenue (Brooks 400).

204.12 Buggering up: Means to spoil or ruin (Partridge 103); here the reporter means that he is doing the job sloppily.

206.1 on the wagon: Slang for no longer drinking alcoholic beverages.

207.3-4 The Ord-Atkinson Aircraft Corp., Blaisedell, Franciana: The manufacturing division of Wedell-Williams Air Service Corp. was located in Patterson, Louisiana (see notes 12.28, 60.4, 168.24).

208.20-21 carbolised: Wiped down with carbolic acid (Phenyl alcohol) in order to disinfect.

209.19 Alphonse's and Renaud's: Brooks identifies these restaurants as Antoine's and Arnaud's, respectively; both are famous New Orleans restaurants (401).

213.16 I guess I can land it all right: Shumann realizes that the problem is not merely one of weight distribution, rather a design flaw. Harrison diagnoses it as not enough elevator to keep the tail of this plane down while landing (165); (see notes 172.17, 174.11, 174.21).

215.8 Cajun: Acadian; loosely, any country person speaking the Acadian dialect (Louisiana: A Guide 686). People of French ancestry who were driven from Nova Scotia by the British in 1755.

216.25-29 he lay on his stomach in the barrel . . . nothing to feel but terrific motion: The reporter's hurtling through the air clinging only to the plane's bodymembers is reminiscent of Quixote's being hurled through the air holding onto his lance, flung by the giant windmill (Miguel De Cervantes, Don Quixote, trans. Peter Motteux [New York: Modern Library, 1930] 40). The reporter will use his body "as a moveable counterweight," pushing himself toward the tail as the airplane slows to land (Harrison 166); (see notes 1734.21, 189.13).

216.26 barrel: The fuselage of the aircraft (see note 217.27).

216.27 bodymembers: Structural   components; bracing, though not cross-bracing (see notes 167.15 and 217.2-3).

216.28 rudderpedals: Pedals which the pilot uses to control the rudder--or the control surface on the trailing edge of the fin which provides directional control (see note 167.15).

216.29 aileron balancerod: An aileron is a control surface, a moveable flap on the trailing edge of a wing, which the pilot uses to bank or turn the airplane.   The balancerod is a "counterweight which keeps the aileron in a neutral position" until pressure is applied through the control stick (see note 174.1); (Harrison 166).

217.2-3 monococque: A system of aircraft construction in which the outer shell or skin of the aircraft carries the stress of flight and landing. Vertical bulkheads formed of structural members are the only reinforcement (Beckford 69; Baughman 120).

217.28-29 He used all the field: Shumann has the same problem landing the plane as Ord did, even after ballasting the airplane with the reporter's body. Because he must keep a smooth current of air flowing over the tail, he can not slow down to land. Rather he makes a high-speed landing using all the runway (Harrison 167). (See notes 174.9, 174.11, 174.21, 189.13, 216.25-29.)

218.24 it aint got an crossbracing: Because it is a monococque (see note 217.2-3).

219.20-21 truck innertube full of sand on a pulley: Shumann will move these weights about to compensate for center of gravity shifts (see note 189.13).

220.11 Lindbergh: Charles Augustus Lindbergh (1902-1974), America's "foremost airman." The son of a Congressman, he dropped out of college to enroll in the flying school of the Lincoln (Nebraska) Standard Aircraft Company. An expert mechanic, he was also soon doing wing-walking and double parachute jumping. In 1923 he bought a Jenny and started barnstroming in the Middle West. He attended U.S. Army Flying School, served in the reserves, and in 1926 and 1927 flew the mail. In 1927 in "The Spirit of St. Louis" he made the first solo non-stop transatlantic flight, between New York and Paris (The National Cyclopaedia of American Biography [New York: White, 1938] 440).

221.21 hop: A flight over a very short distance.

221.25 pass the burble: Move the weights about to offset, primarily, the heaviness of the plane's nose (see note 189.13) and maintain the smooth flow of air over the plane's tail, in other words, to "pass the burble" (see note 174.9).

224.7 Is there crop reduction in the air too?: In his chronicle of the thirties (1939), Frederick Lewis Allen writes that "The New Deal came to the rescue of the farm population with a bill which aimed to raise the prices of the major American farm crops by offering payments to farmers to leave part of their acreage unplanted" (Since Yesterday: The 1930s in America, September 3, 1929-September 3, 1939 [New York: Harper & Row, 1968] 93). "With cotton the method was different; the crop having already been planted, rewards were offered for plowing up part of it (Allen 93-94).

227.5 stickstraddler: Generally, a flyer, the stick referring to the steering mechanism for the plane, which stands up between the pilot's knees. Here Ord seems to be using the term to refer to those who depend on airshows and races for their livelihood.

228.13 writ of replevin: A court order to recover personal property.

228.22 A.A.A.: Though here this stands for the American Aeronautical Association (see P 141), in reality the A.A.A. was the Agricultural Adjustment Administration, the agency in charge of administering crop control (Allen 94). The only two agencies I can find record of which administered aviation at the time were the F.A.A., Federal Aviation Agency, and the C.A.A., Civil Aeronautics Administration (see note 170.7-8).

229.29 Frenchman Despleins: According to Millgate, "Faulkner seems to have combined both De Troyat and Milo Burcham in the figure of the French pilot, Jules Despleins, who apparently does most of his stunts upside down" (140). Burcham was champion upside-down flyer, De Troyat a famous aerobatic champion, on whom the organizers must have counted to pull in the crowds as his name was prominent in publicity for the show.

229.28 darkhorse: A little-known contestant in a race or contest.

231.11 Snap me: Slang for taking someone's picture.

231.14 in-ver-ted spin: A spin, controlled or uncontrolled, in which the airplane is upside down throughout. The tail of the airplane is pointed sharply downward (Frank D. Adams, NASA Aeronautical Dictionary [Washington, DC: US Government Printing Office, 1959] 158).

232.4 unlimited free-for-all: A race not restricted by engine size. The famous Pulitzer race, first held in Garden City, Long Island, in 1920, was a free-for-all for land planes.

232.7-8 land plane speed record: At the time of his death in Patterson, Louisiana, in June of 1934, Jimmy Wedell held this record. During the winter preceding the races in New

Orleans, Wedell had designed and built a "magnificent new racing aircraft" (Roseberry 210). Giving it the number "45," "Wedell loafed around a 100-kilometer closed course at New Orleans at 264.703 m.p.h., setting a world record for a closed-circuit flight by landplane" (Roseberry 210).

232.11 nosed over: Flipped over, end over end.

232.22 monoplane: As opposed to the biplane with its double wing, a plane with a single wing.

234.13 light scattering of burnt paper or feathers: Roger's attempt to make a tight turn around the pylon at such high speed has overstressed the body of the plane, and it is breaking up. Ord had originally refused to replace the plane's engine with a bigger, more powerful one as its owner had requested, at least without some modifications in the body of the plane. He and the plane's owner finally compromised on some changes, and Ord did replace the engine (P 172). Clearly, Ord was right when he told the owner, according to the reporter, "the ship had all the engine then it had any business with" (P 172; see note 172.17).

234.19-23 They said later about the apron that he used the last of his control before the fuselage broke to zoom out of the path of the two aeroplanes behind while he looked down at the closepeopled land and empty lake and made a choice: Cf:

War Birds: The Diary of an Unknown Aviator [Elliot White Springs]: "Stratton got smashed up. He was in a Camel and his machine gun ran away so he crashed to keep from shoting another machine" (62). "Nigger Horn had a crash. He was flying an S.E. and had just gotten off the ground when the engine conked. He was headed straight for the town and couldn't turn back. It looked as if he was going to crash into a crowded street but he stuck his nose down and deliberately dove between two little brick buildings on the edge of the field" (65).

235.4 after the bright plain shape of love: Cf. Light in August. Hightower is thinking of his time in the seminary and of his wife: "And more, worse: that with the learning of it, instead of losing something he had gained, had escaped from something. And that gain had colored the very face and shape of love" (453). Cf. The Hamlet, where Ike's cow is "the intact and escaping shape of love" (190).

236 LOVESONG OF J. A. PRUFROCK (chapter title): Of course, very close to the title of T. S. Eliot's poem "The Love Song of J. Alfred Prufrock."

236.15-16 a police launch was scattering the fleet of small boats: When Kenily crashed into Lake Pontchartrain (see note 299.5) "a Coast Guard boat, several speed boats, a small fisherman's boat, and the Yacht Esso" attempted a rescue (Times-Picayune 18 Feb. 1934: 1).

237.6 dory: a type of flat-bottomed boat, narrow with high sides and a sharp prow; a stable craft for oystermen who stand in these boats and fish for oysters with long tongs.

237.8-9 both wings had reappeared: That the wings had broken off after the tail disintegrated indicates structural failure (Harrison 168).

237.11-16 Shumann had been seen struggling to open the cockpit hatch as though to jump, as though with the intention of trying to open his parachute despite his lack of height)--one of the oystermen claimed that the body had fallen free of the machine: Kenily (see note 299.5) apparently also "leaped" from his plane "in an attempt to save his life" (Times-Picayune 18 Feb. 1934: 2).

237.21 skiffs: A skiff is a flat-bottomed, shallow, open boat with a sharp bow and square stern, used by fishermen (Rene de Kerchove, International Maritime Dictionary [New York: Van Nostrand Reinhold, 1961] 741).

237.22 dinghys: Any small, general-purpose rowboat (The Visual Encyclopedia of Nautical Terms Under Sail [New York: Crown, 1978] 09.01)

237.25 launch: "Small open or half-decked boat with mechanical propulsion, usually employed commercially for various purposes in harbors, estuaries, rivers and occasionally for making short trips in coastal waters" (De Kerchove 437).

239.5-6 as though the reporter actually were sinking slowly away from him into clear and limpid water: Cf. Mayday (1926). Sir Galwyn sees in a stream "one all young and white," and when he looks at her "he was as one sinking from a fever into a soft and bottomless sleep; and he stepped forward into the water and Hunger and Pain went away from him, and as the water touched him it seemed to him that he knelt in a dark room waiting for day" ([Notre Dame: U of Notre Dame P, 1978] 87).

241.15 broke off at the tail: The weight of the sandbag in the rear of the plane may have contributed to the breaking off of the tail when Shumann made the vertical turn (Harrison 169); (see note 189.13).

241.21 dredgeboat: "A vessel or floating structure equipped with excavation machinery, employed in deepening channels and harbors, and removing submarine obstructions such as shoals and bars" (De Kerchove 241).

241.26-27 crabs and gars: Crabs are scavengers, and gars are predators. This would be the blue crab (<u>Callinectes sapidus</u>) which inhabits shallows and brackish estuaries (<u>The Audubon Society Field Guide to North American Seashore Creatures</u> [New York: Knopf, 1981] 629-640). "Gars are long cigar-shaped fishes, olive above, gray below, and with thick . . . diamond-shaped scales. They are predators and have beaklike jaws with sharp, pointed teeth. They frequent large streams and rivers and shallow weedy lakes . . . . They can use atmospheric oxygen and may bask on the surface" (Henry Hill Collins, assembler, <u>Complete Guide to North American Wildlife</u>: <u>Eastern Edition</u> [New York: Harper & Row, 1981] 514-515). The alligator gar, which can grow to 93 inches long, has two rows of large teeth in its upper jaw (Collins 515), and the crabs claws, of course, are sharp pincers (see note 16.9).

242.26-27 the palms along the boulevard began to clash and hiss with a dry wild sound: Cf. <u>The Wild Palms</u>, where the "clashing" and "hissing" of the palms is a repeated image. Charlotte "lay all day long apparently watching the palm fronds clashing with their wild dry bitter sound" (8). "The dark wind still filled with the clashing of invisible palms" (279). Cf. "The Waste Land," T. S. Eliot, where the "dry grass" is "singing" (<u>Collected Poems</u> 87).

247.27-28 midnight bells from town which would signal the beginning of Lent: Carnival is over. It is now Ash Wednesday, the first day of "Lent," "from the Anglo-Saxon <u>Lencten</u>, meaning spring . . . the 40-day period of prayer, penance, and spiritual endeavor in preparation for Easter" (<u>The New Catholic Encyclopedia</u> [New York: McGraw Hill, 1967] 8: 624). "The accumulated evidence of Christian tradition . . . shows without any doubt that the real aim of Lent is, above all else, to prepare men for the celebration of death and Resurrection of Christ," for "reliving the mystery of Redemption," which can only be achieved with "purified mind and heart. The purpose of Lent is to provide that purification by weaning men from sin and selfishness through self-denial and prayer" (<u>Catholic Encyclopedia</u> 635). Lent is celebrated by many Christians with fasting of some sort, often abstinence from one kind of food or another. One of the colors of Carnival (see note 7.10-11), purple, is also the color of Lent (Francis X. Weiser, <u>Handbook of Christian Feasts and Customs</u> [New York: Harcourt, Brace, 1952] 169).

248.21 sidearms and putties: Sidearms are weapons worn at the side--primarily pistols or revolvers. For putties see note 102.22.

252.9-10 <u>I might be a bum and a bastard but I am not out there in that lake</u>: Cf. <u>The Sound and the Fury</u>. Quentin is thinking, "any live man is better than any dead man" (125).

258.21 in case they do . . . . around out there: The ellipses here stand for "fuck". Faulkner has crossed through "muck" and noted in the margin--"Period In each letter in 'fuck'."

262.24 jalousies: "In Louisiana, the common two-battened outdoor blind" (City Guide 409). A louvered shutter.

263.1 swampland dyked away: Swamps serve as catch-basins for overflow water and rainfall; thus if they are "dyked away from the stream because of which they came to exist" (P 263), then they are reclaimed, transformed into dry land. As some suspected at the time and as we now know, this kind of tampering with the wetlands has severe environmental repercussions. The river is more likely to flood its banks if the swamps no longer exist to catch the overflow. Also, when wetlands are destroyed the fishing industry suffers, as marshes serve as a kind of nursery, a protected environment, for many species of sea life.

266.5 cathedral clock: The clock in the tower of the St. Louis Cathedral, which faces Jackson Square in the French Quarter (see note 57.8).

267.19 saltmarsh: This would be coastal marsh, the water salty or brackish as opposed to fresh; the vegetation characteristic of a saltmarsh is salt grass, cord grass, black rush, and mangrove (Fred B. Kniffen, <u>Louisiana</u>: <u>Its</u> <u>Land and People</u> [Baton Rouge: Louisiana State UP 1968] 79).

267.21 saltgrass: (<u>Distichlis spicata</u>) "A short perennial grass of brackish and saline marsh. It forms dense stands on slightly elevated areas such as bayou and lake banks, ridges, and soil deposits and is abundant all along the coast . . . . The plant is an important contributor to the detrital cycle, which provides nutrients to estuarine organisms" (Chabreck and Condrey 32); (see note 16.9).

267.22-29 they began to pass the debris, the silent imperishable monument tranquil in the bright sun--old carbodies without engines or wheels, the old engines and wheels without bodies; . . . the blanched sun which was so white itself that for a time Jiggs saw no bones at all: Cf. Ezekiel 37:1-5: "The hand of the Lord was upon me, and carried me out in the spirit of the Lord, and set me down in the midst of the valley which <u>was</u> full of bones./ And caused me to pass by them round about: and, behold, <u>there were</u> very many in the open valley; and, lo, <u>they were</u> very dry./ And he said unto me, Son of man, can these bones live? And I answered, O Lord God, thou knowest./ Again he said to me, Prophesy upon these bones, and say unto them, O ye dry bones, hear the word of the Lord./ Thus saith the Lord God unto these bones; Behold, I will cause breath to enter into you, and ye shall live." Surely Faulkner was thinking of the "stony rubbish" the "heap of broken images, where the sun beats" in Eliot's "Waste Land" (Collected Poems 69); perhaps also of "the valley of ashes" of Fitzgerald's The Great Gatsby ([New York: Scribner's, 1925] 23). The passage is also reminiscent of a war-ruined landscape, as in War Birds [Elliot White Springs]. "I was down right on the ground but saw very few dead bodies but any number of dead horses. The ground was all pockmarked and what little vegetation remained was a light straw color from the gas. Further down I saw the Huns using gas, a thin layer of brownish green stuff was drifting slowly along the ground from a trench about three hundred yards long. But no men were to be seen anywhere. Only dead horses and tanks" (154).

270.11 centaur: Half man, half horse.

271.27-28 He's been white to me: He has treated me decently; he has been honest and fair with me.

272.27 the balls: The three silver balls denoting the pawn shop.

273.25-26 pulp magazines of war stories in the air: Like Sky Birds, Over the Top, Navy Stories, Dare-Devil Aces, War Birds, War Stories, Wings, Air Adventure, Battle Birds. Aviation pulps, especially popular in the thirties, included factual data on aircraft, maneuvers, air battles, dictionaries of aviation terminology, plans for building model aircraft, flying lessons, and lots of pictures (Tony Goodstone, ed., The Pulps: Fifty Years of American Pop Culture [New York: Chelsea, 1970] 45-56, and plates 21-28).

275.20 Hisso Standard: "The Standard Aircraft Company of Plainfield, New Jersey, had developed a two-place trainer similar to the Jenny--but, in fact, its aerodynamic superior--only to have it phased out during the War when its Hall-Scott engine developed a nasty habit of catching fire in mid-air . . . . Once re-equipped with Hispano-Suiza engines, they became the most cherished of the aircraft in which the gypsy barnstormers plied their haphazard trade in the 1920's." This plane was too costly for most flyers (O'Neil 28).

275.25 cracked it up: Slang for wrecked it.

276.20-25 She was a orphan, see; her older sister that was married sent for her to come live with them when her folks died: Cf. Light in August. Lena Grove's background is similar: "When she was twelve years old her father and mother died in the same summer . . . McKinley, the brother, arrived in a wagon . . . The brother was twenty years her senior (2-3). As Laverne escapes with Roger, Lena, pregnant, escapes through an open window.

277.8 twotime: "To double-cross someone, esp. in affairs of the heart; specif., to deceive one's sweetheart or spouse by being unfaithful" (Wentworth 559).

278.11 stalking horse: Slang for the one taking the risks or preparing the way for someone else.

279.8-21 It started out to be a tragedy. A good orthodox Italian tragedy. You know: one Florentine falls in love with another Florentine's wife and spends three acts fixing it up to put the bee on the second Florentine . . .: Robert Browning's "dramatic romance," "The Statue and the Bust" (1855), set in Florence, is the story of the Great-Duke Ferdinand and a lady with whom he falls in love on the day of her wedding to another man. Though she marries, she and the Duke plot to run away together. But time passes; they procrastinate; their plans are never realized.

279.12 put the bee on: Perhaps this is slang for trick or dupe, related to sting, which is an elaborate hoax.

280.10-11 sage dusters out of the old Southern country thought: Like dusters or brooms made from bundles of sage, actually sedge. According to Brown, sedge is any of various species of the genus Andropogon, tall grass, light green in summer and brown in winter, which stands in abandoned fields or open spaces along the edges of swamps (171).

281.13 wingovers: The plane enters "a steep climbing turn until speed decays to near the stall, at which point the nose is allowed to fall while the turn is continued through 180 degrees." The wingover and vertical turn are "approximately those executed by Roger Shumann in the last moments of his life" (Harrison 169).

281.18 ragtag and bobend: This expression usually runs-- "ragtag and bobtail," meaning rubble. Perhaps Faulkner is thinking of Prufrock's "buttends" (<u>Collected Poems</u> 14).

285 THE SCAVENGERS (chapter title): Cf. <u>Blue Voyage</u>, Conrad Aiken: "'Scavengers!' she cried. 'That's what we are. Devourers of the dead; devourers of ourselves. Prometheus and the vulture are one in the same'" ([New York: Scribner's, 1927] 262).

289.3 putting himself away: Killing himself.

289.28-29 laying her: Slang for having sex with.

290.5 Jekyll and Hyde: Of the "Strange case of Dr. Jekyll and Mr. Hyde," Robert Louis Stevenson's 1886 story. Dr. Jekyll was an essentially good man who was, nevertheless, fascinated by the idea of evil and developed a drug which transformed him into the evil Mr. Hyde. A Jekyll and Hyde is anyone who seems to harbor two distinct personalities in one body.

290.26 bellyaching: Slang meaning to complain loudly, to whine.

291.22 purity squad: Slang for the sanitary squad which picks up and disposes of the dead--animals and human.

292.27 a game blows up in your face: Slang for something which no longer pays off.

292.29 hustle up: Hustle means "to be active or energetic in earning money by one's wit" (Wentworth 277).

292.30 another game that you can beat: Another way to win or earn some money.

293.1 to sweat: To work hard at something (Wentworth 530).

293.2 something in the sock: Money saved, a sock being, among members of the underworld in the thirties, any receptacle like a bag, box, or safe where money was kept (Wentworth 500).

293.2 when the snow flies: Slang for when the times are hard, as in winter.

295.10 Bienville Hotel: Cleanth Brooks has identified this hotel: "One of the more curious place names in Pylon is that of the Bienville Hotel. In <u>Pylon</u> it is situated on a side street and is shabby and raffish in atmosphere (295). But in the 1930s there was in New Orleans an actual Bienville Hotel, not as prestigious as the St. Charles or as large as the Roosevelt, but new, clean, eminently respectable, and situated on St. Charles Ave. very near Lee Circle. Faulkner was probably unaware that a Bienville Hotel actually existed. I suspect he simply chose 'Bienville' as a suitable name for a New Orleans hostelry. It is the actual name of a street in the Vieux Carré" (401).

295.14-15 Turkish Bath: The process by which one sits in a super-heated room, perspires profusely, and then is massaged. In the sleazier parts of towns, these places were often actually houses of prostitution.

296.8 Myron, Ohio: There is no Myron in Ohio. Charles W. Kenily, the pilot who crashed into Lake Pontchartrain during the actual airshow and whose body was never found, was from Marion, Ohio (<u>Times-Picayune</u> 16 Feb. 1934: 3); (see note 299.5).

296.11 doc: Slang term used in direct address for an unknown fellow.

297.28 a tatting Christmas gift: Handmade, knotted lace.

298.5-7 it came over into what they thought was position and the sound of the engine died for a time: Although in _Pylon_ a wreath is being dropped, Captain Merle Nelson's (see note 52.15-16) ashes were scattered by Milo Burcham (see note 27.15) "who cut the engine of his plane and went into a glide as he scattered the ashes" (_Times-Picayune_ 18 Feb. 1934: 2).

299.5 AVIATOR'S BODY RESIGNED TO LAKE GRAVE: As Millgate notes (_Achievement_ 140), Charles W. Kenily of Marion, Ohio, crashed into Lake Pontchartrain when the lines of his jumper's parachute became entangled with the plane's tail (_Times-Picayune_ 18 Feb. 1934: 1). As subsequent newspaper reports indicate, Kenily's body was never found (_Times-Picayune_ 19, 20 Feb. 1934).

300.26 Something is going to happen to me: Cf. _Sanctuary_. Temple says, "Something is going to happen to me" before she is raped (122). Cf. _Light in August_, where Joe Christmas says, "Something is going to happen to me" (97, 110).

304.19 cenotaph: Means empty tomb, and is used to refer to a monument for those who die away from home and whose bodies cannot be recovered, like the famous Whitehall monument to Britain's war dead (Edwin Radford, _To Coin a Phrase: A Dictionary of Origins_, rev. and ed. Alan Smith [London: Hutchinson, 1973] 24).

304.21 bungalow: A single-story house; the equivalent in the twenties and thirties of the ranch houses which have proliferated in subdivisions in our time. In Faulkner, bungalows are generally the cheap or dingy, in-town residences of the defeated. For instance, Horace Benbow retreats to his bungalow and Belle after losing Goodwin's case in Sanctuary. In Light in August, Hightower lives in a "brown, unpainted and unobtrusive bungalow" (52), as do the Hineses (322).

304.21 stoops: A broad platform step at the entrance to a house (Saylor 165).

304.21-22 port-cochères: A shelter for vehicles outside an entrance doorway (Pevsner 396).

304.22 flat gables: A gable is the "triangular upper portion of a wall at the end of a pitched roof" (Pevsner 187).

304.22 bays: A bay is a bay window or the upright portion of a building contained between adjacent supports or columns (Saylor 118).

306.25-27 nothing is worth anything but peace, peace, peace: Horace Benbow, in Flags in the Dust, wants "quiet and dull peace" after having come home from the war (164).

307.5-7 that you were born bad and could not help it or did not think you were going to try to help it: Cf. The Sound and the Fury. Miss Quentin says, "I'm bad and I'm going to hell and I don't care" (235).

307.30 I have decided now: Cf. Soldiers' Pay. Margaret Powers thinks, "Freedom comes with the decision: it does not wait for the act" (301).

312.19 fumed oak: Oak furniture which has been exposed to fumes of ammonia in an air-tight chamber before polishing, the wood a greyish-brown color, which gradually fades "to a repellant hue of yellowish brown" (John Gloag, A Short History of Furniture [London: Allen and Unwin, 1969] 345). This process was popular at the end of the 19th and during the early 20th centuries (see note 11.28).

Works Cited

Adams, Frank D. NASA Aeronautical Dictionary. Washington, DC: US Government Printing Office, 1959.

Adams, Richard P. Faulkner: Myth and Motion. Princeton: Princeton UP, 1968.

Aiken, Conrad. Blue Voyage. New York: Scribner's, 1927.

_____. Nocturne of Remembered Spring. Boston: Four Seas, 1917.

Allen, Frederick Lewis. Since Yesterday: The 1930s in America, September 3, 1929-September 3, 1939. New York: Harper & Row, 1968.

The American Heritage Dictionary of the English Dictionary. 1978 ed.

Anderson, Sherwood. Marching Men. Cleveland: P of Case Western Reserve U, 1972.

_____. Poor White. New York: Huebsch, 1920.

_____. Triumph of the Egg. New York: Huebsch, 1921.

_____. Winesburg, Ohio. New York: Huebsch, 1919.

The Audubon Society Field Guide to North American Seashore Creatures. New York: Knopf, 1981.

Barbusse, Henri. Under Fire: The Story of a Squad. New York: Dutton, 1917.

Baughman, Harold E. Baughman's Aviation Dictionary and Reference Guide. Glendale, CA: Aero, 1940.

Beckford, L. L. An A.B.C. of Aeronautics. London: Cassell, 1957.

Berman, Louis. The Glands Regulating Personality: A Study of the Glands of Secretion in Relation to the Types of Human Nature. New York: MacMillan, 1922.

Barrey, Lester V. and Melvin Van Den Bark, comps. The American Thesaurus of Slang, 2nd ed. New York: Crowell, 1953.

Barthelme, Helen. "Pylon: The Doomed Quest. A Critical and Textual Study of Faulkner's Neglected Allegory." Diss. U of Texas at Austin, 1976.

Bleikasten, André. "Pylon, Ou L'enfer des Signes." Études Anglaises 29(1976): 437-447.

Blotner, Joseph. Faulkner: A Biography. New York: Random House, 1974.

_____ and Frederick Gwyn, eds. Faulkner in the University: Class Conferences at the University of Virginia 1957-1958. Charlottesville: UP of Virginia, 1959.

_____. "Notes for Pylon." William Faulkner: Novels 1930-1935. New York: Library of America, 1985.

_____, ed. The Selected Letters of William Faulkner. New York: Random House, 1977.

_____. William Faulkner's Library--A Catalog. Charlottesville: UP of Virginia, 1964.

Brooks, Cleanth. William Faulkner: Toward Yoknapatawpha and Beyond. New Haven: Yale UP, 1978.

Brown, Calvin S. A Glossary of Faulkner's South. New Haven: Yale UP, 1976.

Bulfinch, Thomas. Bulfinch's Mythology. New York: Crowell, 1913.

Calasibetta, Charlotte. Fairchild's Dictionary of Fashion. New York: Fairchild Publications, 1975.

Carter, Hodding, Jr., ed. The Past as Prelude: New Orleans 1718-1968. New Orleans: Tulane UP, 1968.

Cervantes, Miguel de. Don Qixote. New York: Hogarth, 1900.

_____. Don Quixote. New York: The Modern Library, 1930.

Chabreck, R. H. and R. E. Condrey. Common Vascular Plants of the Louisiana Marsh. Baton Rouge: LSU Center for Wetland Resources, 1979.

The Collector's Encyclopedia: Victorian/Art Deco. London: Collins, 1974.

Collins, Henry Hall, assembler. Complete Guide to North American Wildlife: Eastern Edition. New York: Harper & Row, 1981.

The Compact Edition of the Oxford English Dictionary. 1971.

cummings, e. e. Complete Poems: 1913-1962. New York: Harcourt Brace Jovanovich, 1972.

De Kerchove, Rene. _International Maritime Dictionary_. New York: Van Nostrand Reinhold, 1961.

Dickens, Charles. _A Christmas Carol_. New York: Putnam's, 1900.

Dos Passos, John. _Manhattan Transfer_. New York: Somerset, 1925.

_____. _U.S.A._ New York: Modern Library, 1937.

Doxat, John. _The Book of Drinking_. London: Triune, 1973.

Eliot, T. S. _Collected Poems_: _1909-1935_. New York: Harcourt, Brace, 1936.

_____. "The Hollow Men." _Dial_ 78(1925).

_____. _Prufrock and Other Observations_. London: Egoist, 1917.

_____. _The Waste Land_. New York: Boni & Liveright, 1922.

Encyclopedia Americana. 1984 ed.

Encyclopaedia Britannica. 1980 ed.

Faulkner, William. _Absalom, Absalom!_ New York: Random House, 1936.

_____. _Elmer_. Ed. Dianne Cox. _Mississippi Quarterly_ 36(1983): 337-460.

_____. _Flags in the Dust_. New York: Random House, 1973.

_____. _The Hamlet_. New York: Random House, 1940.

_____. _Helen_: _A Courtship and Mississippi Poems_. Ed. Carvel Collins. New Orleans and Oxford MS: Tulane U and Yoknapatawpha P, 1981.

_____. "An Introduction to _The Sound and the Fury_." Ed. James B. Meriwether. _Mississippi Quarterly_ 26(1973): 410-415.

_____. "An Introduction for _The Sound and the Fury_." Ed. James B. Meriwether. _Southern Review_ 8(1972): 705-710.

_____. _Light in August_. New York: Harrison Smith and Robert Haas, 1932.

_____. _The Marble Faun and A Green Bough_. New York: Random House, 1965.

_____. _Mayday_. Notre Dame: U of Notre Dame P, 1978.

_____. _Mosquitoes_. New York: Boni & Liveright, 1927.

_____. _Pylon_. New York: Harrison Smith and Robert Haas, 1935.

_____. "Raid." _The Saturday Evening Post_ 3 Nov. 1934.

_____. _Sanctuary_. New York: Modern Library, 1932.

_____ and William Spratling. _Sherwood Anderson & Other Famous Creoles_. Austin: U of Texas P, 1966.

_____. _Soldiers' Pay_. New York: Boni & Liveright, 1926.

_____. _The Sound and the Fury_. New York: Jonathan Cape and Harrison Smith, 1929.

_____. "The Unvanquished." _The Saturday Evening Post_ 14 Nov. 1936.

_____. _The Unvanquished_. New York: Random House, 1938.

_____. _Vision in Spring_. Austin: U of Texas P, 1984.

_____. _The Wild Palms_. New York: Random House, 1939.

Federal Writers' Program, Lyle Saxon, state sup. _Louisiana: A Guide to the State_. New York: Hastings, 1941.

Federal Writers' Project, Lyle Saxon, dir. _New Orleans City Guide_. Boston: Houghton Mifflin, 1938.

Fitch, James M. "Creole Architecture 1718-1860: The Rise and Fall of a Great Tradition." _Past as Prelude: New Orleans 1718-1968_. Ed. Hodding Carter, Jr. New Orleans: Tulane UP, 1968.

Fitzgerald, F. Scott. _The Great Gatsby_. New York: Scribner's, 1925.

Frazer, Sir James. _The Golden Bough: A Study in Magic and Religion_. New York: MacMillan, 1922.

Freud, Sigmund. _A General Introduction to Psycho-Analysis: A Course of Twenty-Eight Lectures Delivered at the University of Vienna_. New York: Liveright 1926; rpt. 1935.

Gidley, Mick. "Another Psychologist, a Physiologist, and William Faulkner." _Ariel_ 2(1971): 78-86.

Gloag, John. A Short History of Furniture. London: Allen and Unwin, 1969.

Glut, Donald F. The Dracula Book. Metuchen, NJ: Scarecrow, 1975.

Goodstone, Tony, ed. The Pulps: Fifty Years of American Pop Culture. New York: Chelsea, 1970.

Goreau, Laurraine, "Mardi Gras." The Past as Prelude: New Orleans 1718-1968. Ed. Hodding Carter, Jr. New Orleans: Tulane UP, 1968.

Greene, Wilhelmina F. and Hugo L. Blomquist. Flowers of the South, Native and Exotic. Chapel Hill: U of North Carolina P, 1953.

Hall, Calvin S. A Primer of Freudian Psychology. New York: New American Library, 1954.

Harrison, Robert. Aviation Lore in Faulkner. Amsterdam: Benjamins, 1985.

Hawthorne, Nathaniel. The Marble Faun. New York: New American Library, 1954.

Johnson, Hugh. The International Book of Trees. New York: Simon and Schuster, 1973.

Johnson, Phil. "Good Time Town." Past as Prelude: New Orleans 1718-1968. Ed. Hodding Carter, Jr. New Orleans, Tulane UP, 1968.

Jordan, Peter. "April Fool!" Notes on Mississippi Writers 12(1979): 17-22.

Joyce, James. Ulysses. New York: Modern Library, 1934.

Katz, Ephraim. The Film Encyclopedia. New York: Crowell, 1979.

Keats, John. "The Eve of St. Agnes." The Complete Poetical Works of John Keats. London: Oxford UP, 1929. 212-229.

King, Grace. New Orleans: The Place and Its People. New York: MacMillan, 1911.

Kniffen, Fred B. Louisiana: Its Land and People. Baton Rouge: Louisiana State UP, 1968.

LaFarge, Oliver. Laughing Boy. Cambridge, MA.: Houghton Mifflin, 1929.

Lewis, Sinclair. The Trail of the Hawk. New York: Harcourt, Brace, 1915.

Maloney, Joan. Art and Architecture at Lakefront Airport. Pamphlet in commemoration of fiftieth anniversary of Lakefront Airport, 1984.

Mast, Gerald. A Short History of the Movies, 3rd ed. Indianapolis: Bobbs-Merrill, 1981.

Mayer, Ralph. A Dictionary of Art Terms and Techniques. New York: Crowell, 1967.

McElrath, Joseph R., Jr. "Pylon: The Portrait of a Lady." Mississippi Quarterly 27(1974): 277-290.

Meriwether, James B., ed. Essays, Speeches and Public Letters by William Faulkner. New York: Random House, 1966.

_____ and Michael Millgate, eds. Lion in the Garden: Interviews with William Faulkner, 1926-1962. New York: Random House, 1968.

_____. "The Old Roman and His Vase." The Faulkner Newsletter & Yoknapatawpha Review 2(1982): 2, 4.

Millgate, Michael. The Achievement of William Faulkner. New York: Random House, 1966.

The National Cyclopaedia of Biography. New York: White, 1938.

The New Catholic Encyclopedia. New York: McGraw Hill, 1967.

New York Times Biographical Service.

O'Neil, Paul. Barnstormers and Speed Kings. Alexandria, VA: Time-Life, 1981.

Partridge, Eric, comp. A Dictionary of Slang and Unconventional English, 7th ed. New York: MacMillan, 1970.

Pearl, Anita. Dictionary of Popular Slang. New York: David, 1980.

Pevsner, Nikolaus, et.al. A Dictionary of Modern American Architecture. Woodstock, NY: Overlook, 1976.

Placzek, Adolf K., ed. MacMillan Encyclopedia of Architecture. New York: Free Press, 1982.

Pound, Ezra. Lustra. New York: Knopf, 1917.

_____. Selected Poems. New York: New Directions, 1957.

Radford, Edwin. To Coin a Phrase: A Dictionary of Origins, rev. and ed. by Alan Smith. London: Hutchinson, 1973.

Roberts, W. Adolphe. Lake Pontchartrain. New York: Bobbs-Merril, 1946.

Robinson, Anthony, ed. The Encyclopedia of American Aircraft. New York: Galahad, 1979.

Robinson, Jerry. The Comics: Illustrated History of Comic Strip Art. New York: Putnam's, 1974.

Roseberry, C. R. The Challenging Skies. New York: Arno, 1980.

Rothenstein, Sir John, ed. New International Encyclopedia of Art. New York: Greystone, 1970.

Ruppersburg, Hugh M. Voice and Eye in Faulkner's Fiction. Athens: U of Georgia P, 1983.

Saxon, Lyle. Fabulous New Orleans. New York: Century, 1928.

Saylor, Henry H. Dictionary of Architecture. New York: Wiley, 1952.

Seltzer, Leon E., ed. The Columbia Lippincott Gazetteer of the World. New York: Columbia UP, 1962.

Serafin, Joan M. Faulkner's Use of the Classics. Ann Arbor: UMI Research Press, 1983.

Shakespeare, William. The Complete Works. Baltimore: Penguin, 1969.

Shelley, Mary. Frankenstein; or The Modern Prometheus. New York: Harrison Smith and Robert Haas, 1934.

Sienkiewicz, H. Quo Vadis. Boston: Little Brown, 1897.

[Springs, Elliot White]. War Birds: The Diary of an Unknown Aviator. London: Temple, 1966.

Stevenson, Robert Louis. The Strange Case of Dr. Jekyll and Mr. Hyde. New York: Grosset & Dunlap, 1900.

Sturgis, Russell. A Dictionary of Architecture and Building. New York: MacMillan, 1901.

Tallant, Robert. <u>Mardi Gras</u>. Garden City, NY: Doubleday, 1948.

<u>Times</u>-<u>Picayune</u> (New Orleans) 14-20 Feb. 1934.

Toole, John Kennedy. <u>A Confederacy of Dunces</u>. Baton Rouge: Louisiana State UP, 1980.

Vickery, John B. "William Faulkner and Sir Philip Sydney?" <u>Modern Language Notes</u> 70(1955): 344-350.

<u>The Visual Encyclopedia of Nautical Terms Under Sail</u>. New York: Crown, 1978.

Volpe, Edmond. <u>A Reader's Guide to William Faulkner</u>. New York: Farrar, Straus and Giroux, 1964.

Vorderman, Don. <u>The Great Air Races</u>. Garden City, NY: Doubleday, 1969.

Weiser, Francis X. <u>Handbook of Christian Feasts and Customs</u>: <u>The Year of the Lord in Liturgy and Folklore</u>. New York: Harcourt, Brace, 1952.

Wentworth, Harold and Stuart Flexner, comps. <u>Dictionary of American Slang</u>. New York: Crowell, 1975.

Wittenberg, Judith. <u>The Transfiguration of Biography</u>. Lincoln: U of Nebraska P, 1979.

Yarwood, Doreen. <u>Costume of the Western World</u>. New York: St. Martin's, 1980.

Zim, Herbert. <u>Parachutes</u>. New York: Harcourt, Brace, 1942.